Stranger Places

by

Sandra Peterson Ramirez

and

td Whittle

Thirteen Ways Press

Stranger Places

Published by Thirteen Ways Press, First Print Edition
Publisher Website: **thirteenways.com.au**

Copyright © Sandra Peterson Ramirez and td Whittle, 2017
Author Website: **www.liketellingthetruth.com**

The cover image is from a photo taken by the authors in the
West Texas desert.

The quote on the opening page is an excerpt from Lewis
Burke Frumkes' interview with Kazuo Ishiguro in *The
Writer*, volume 114, number 5, May 2001, collected in
Conversations with Kazuo Ishiguro, p. 189.

For all the Avas in the universe, wherever you find yourselves.

"There was another life that I might have had, but I am having this one."

- Kazuo Ishiguro

One

"We don't want your trash here," the clerk snapped at Ava and shoved the recycling bag back to her. Ava grabbed the bag just before it slid off the counter.

"It's not trash," Ava explained. "It's empty cans and bottles. I guess you're not one of the shops that serves as a recycling center? Many California businesses—"

"California? Boy, are you lost!" The clerk laughed in a way that Ava thought derisive and, without another word, returned to stocking the shelves behind the sales counter.

Bewildered, Ava didn't push negotiations further. Instead, she nodded once, picked up her bag, and walked straight out the door, forgetting to buy something to eat. Without the refund money from the cans and bottles, dinner would be meager, which wouldn't have mattered if every other meal this week had not been meager. She counted what was left of the cash she'd earned clipping hedges in a suburban garden, which came to almost sixty dollars. She would need to save most of that to pay for a place to shower and sleep tonight. *At least I have some money,* she thought, *and it's not cold out.* She searched for a third thing to be grateful for but came up empty.

She contemplated dinner while loitering outside the grocery store. The town looked lightly populated, at least judging from the few people outside. There were no cars, either. It was so quiet that her stomach growling was the loudest sound Ava could hear. She glanced up and down the broad main street, spotting places to buy food: a diner up the road and across from where she stood, and a gas station right next door, with a sign advertising chips and candy bars. She knew the grocery store would be cheaper than either of those.

Ava interpreted her stomach's growling as a plea for a steak with fries and salad, but she didn't let herself think about when she could've afforded such a meal. Those days were long gone, at least until she reached home, which she might have done by now if she hadn't ditched her ride with a trucker to come to this pokey desert town. Now, she could not remember why she'd done that and wondered what she'd been thinking.

As she lingered on the sidewalk, gathering her courage to go back into the shop and face the clerk again, a man opened the door and held it for her. She hadn't noticed him approach and chided herself for not being more aware of her surroundings. She paused at the doorway and took a deep breath, noticing the faint odors of sandalwood soap and marijuana. Ava took a better look at the guy: mid-thirties with a hippie vibe, but upscale, and not bad looking if you like the white dude with dreads thing.

"Going in?" He and the Irish setter next to him both gave her a questioning head tilt.

Ava nodded.

"You can leave your bag out here, and your pack too. Your belongings will be safe."

She arched a brow at him.

"I promise," the stranger said.

Ava sighed, but she didn't want another hassle with the locals. She dropped the bag just outside the door, kept her travel pack on, and went inside. Maybe people thought she was homeless, seeing her lugging a huge backpack with a bedroll secured to it, along with a bag of jangling cans and bottles. Also, she'd not had a proper shower in several days. Maybe they didn't like street people in this town.

As she browsed the aisles, choosing what kind of chips she wanted to go with her quart of orange drink, Ava listened to Dreadlocks and Rude Clerk talking at the front of the store. The conversation was perplexing and just loud enough for her to hear.

"She doesn't belong here," the clerk said.

"That may be true, but the one who does belong here is away."

"That doesn't matter!"

"I think it might."

An awkward silence replaced their arguing as Ava approached the counter, eager to pay and get out of the store as quickly as possible. Her groceries looked wretched, even to her, and she was accustomed to wretched. She'd been distracted by the conversation at the register, which was obviously about her, and she was confused by the unfamiliar packages on the store shelves. She'd grabbed items bearing familiar names: a can of Hi-C Orange Drink, a bag of Fritos, a tin of bean dip, a packet of Hostess Twinkies, and two Hershey's Milk Chocolate Bars. She couldn't figure out why all the labels looked so peculiar. Ava stared at her chips and considered the little cowboy in the Frito Kid shirt, who peered at her sideways while licking his upper lip. Creepy.

"How much do I owe you?" Ava asked. She gave the clerk a deadpan stare, waiting for her to ring up the sale, and tried to figure out who the young woman resembled.

Up close, Ava realized that the clerk was probably around her age, at least twenty, and adorable, physically speaking. The clerk was short, maybe an inch or two over five feet, and curvy. Her hair was a glossy black bob, mostly hidden under the red and white polka-dot scarf she'd tied to her head. Bangs curled across the dusky skin of her forehead, drooping into a pair of bright green eyes that were played to their best effect with thick black liner. Her mouth was a full, perfect bow, its natural pout amplified by lollipop-red lipstick. She wore a white cotton blouse and plain blue jeans. Her badge said, "Hi, I'm Jasmine!"

As Ava reflected on what exotic ancestry might produce such a girl, Jasmine snapped at her again: "You know what? Your snacks are on the house." She pushed Ava's bag of groceries across the counter to her, just as she'd shoved her recyclables back to her earlier.

"What do you mean 'on the house'?" Ava asked.

"'On the house' means free. We're holding a giveaway for tall blonde chicks wearing sky-blue travel packs. It's your lucky day. Now please take all your bags and go." Jasmine fluttered her hand in the direction of Ava's recycling bag, visible through the shop door.

Ava was silent for a moment, clutching a ten-dollar bill that she'd dug out of her jeans pocket, and unsure what to do next. She was used to being disliked, but Jasmine's blatant hostility mystified her. She looked at the brown paper bag on the counter, reading the words "Zoom-the-Moon Grocers" which were looped around a 1950s-style spaceship logo. It reminded her of *The Jetsons*. She set her money on the counter and tilted the bag to examine it.

She could feel Jasmine and Dreadlocks staring at her. Worn down from cumulative hunger and fatigue, and disconcerted by her experiences so far in this place that was not California, Ava took a moment before looking up again. She had the urge to grab her groceries and run like a child or a thief but then realized that running was out of the question. She was too depleted. *Besides*, she thought, *I am neither of those.*

Instead, she sighed and stared back at the strangers, scowling in a way she hoped was vaguely menacing and arching her left brow. "Whatever your problem is with me, I am a legal citizen and an adult. I have the right to be here, or anywhere else I want to be, as far as I know."

She was looking right at Jasmine, but it was the man who replied. "Forgive me if I'm mistaken," he said, "but you seem like you need a place to stay, a hand maybe?"

Her scowl intensified. Ava had been perfecting the scowl ever since puberty for the same reason a cat puffs out its fur: to appear bigger to would-be attackers.

"I don't need charity," she answered, before confronting Jasmine directly, "and I don't take candy from strangers, thank you. I'd like to pay for my dinner—my snacks, I mean. What do I owe you?"

Jasmine didn't answer, except to roll her eyes and shrug.

"Here, this should cover it," Ava said. She pushed her ten-dollar bill across the counter and turned to leave.

It was the man again whose voice stopped her. "Look, don't mind us. It's just that we don't get many strangers from the desert here, even passing through." He smiled at Ava, and she took in his tanned skin, sparkling eyes, and shiny white teeth. He looked like a toothpaste commercial for ganja-loving surfer dudes.

"We want to be good hosts," he continued. "How about giving us a chance to extend our hospitality?"

"Seriously, Jack, she should go," the clerk hissed, looking away from Ava and back to Dreadlocks. "It's fine to feed her, but she shouldn't stay here."

"I am not a stray cat," Ava said, a hiss in her own voice that surprised her. "And I'm standing right in front of you, so please stop talking about me as if I were invisible."

Dreadlocks, who was apparently named Jack, ignored Jasmine's comment and smiled warmly at Ava. Ava wondered if he was the town mayor or some other official, as he had that air of casual authority that you sometimes see in laidback but quietly in-charge types.

"Listen up, okay? If you take a right out the door and walk to the end of the block, and then turn right again, you'll reach the entrance to the RV park halfway down the alley. Walk under the arch and turn right again, and then head to the back of the block. You'll find a silver camper back there, a mini Airstream. You are welcome to stay there. The owners are . . ."

The lengthy pause combined with an unsubtle exchange of glances between the irritable clerk and the possible mayor made Ava wonder if his next words would be, "recently deceased and buried right where you're standing," but eventually he coughed up less spectacular news.

". . . on an indefinite holiday."

Ava considered the offer, which sounded much better than lugging her stuff around for another hour or longer while looking for affordable lodging. "I do need a place to crash tonight. I can pay, you know. Despite what you may think of me, I'm not broke," Ava said, casting a sideways glare at Jasmine. "Well, not totally broke."

"That's not necessary," Jack continued. "The owners are generous women. They'd be happy to know you made use of the place, kept it safe and lived-in for them. There's food in the fridge at the RV office—that's just to the left of the park entrance—and a shower block over by the pool, which is near the camper. It's all yours."

Jasmine opened her mouth as if to issue more warnings or argue with him, but Jack's glance shut her down. "Trust me, Jasmine. I will take care of this. Okay?" He winked at the clerk, who once again rolled her eyes dramatically, but held her tongue.

Ava didn't care. Let the snotty clerk think and say what she liked, but she'd made up her mind. She wanted to stay the night here, and this fellow Jack was offering hospitality. What else did she need to know? Ava thanked them both before picking up her grocery bag and heading for the door.

She looked back just once, at Jasmine, which was just long enough for her to make the connection to a figure she'd only ever seen in souvenir shops. Then, as if a thought bubble had appeared over her head, bypassing her brain, Ava blurted out: "Boop-Oop-a-Doop!" It was an anachronism that she'd never used, never having met a real-life Betty Boop. For Ava, the singsong phrase suggested beautiful things like birthday cakes, sparklers, bubble baths, and satin pillows. Ava smiled to herself as she pushed the door open to the sound of tinkling bells and Jack's laughter.

Later, she would wonder what had possessed her to accept such an offer from a stranger. Other than hitching rides, it had become her custom to rebuff help. She was independent by nature and committed to completing this trip relying on her skills and resources. Had it made a difference to know that two women owned the Airstream? Maybe. Probably.

After locating the Airstream and dropping her things inside, she headed to the office trailer. A sign posted on the door informed her that she was a guest at the Infinite Express RV Park. As promised, there was food in the refrigerator and a note that read "Free Eats! Help Yourself!" Everything in the fridge had been individually wrapped or packaged and clearly labeled. Ava took one of the brown paper bags lying on the counter and packed it with sandwiches, potato salad, orange juice, milk, fruit, vegetables, and a family-sized pie.

Despite Jack's insistence that payment was unnecessary, Ava decided to leave some cash in the drawer of the office desk. She laughed when she saw the taped-on label reading "CASH DRAWER" and figured they must have a low crime rate around these parts. When she opened the drawer, she found a stack of unused envelopes bound by a rubber band, alongside a second pile of envelopes with cash stuffed into them. Ava looked at the handwriting on the envelopes and noticed that each one said "Space 8," the space in which the Airstream was parked. She picked up the packets to look for dates but found none, so she decided to look at the money itself. Ava pulled out a few bills and scrutinized them, discovering only common currency bearing dates from the 1980s through the early 2000s.

After putting everything back as it had been, she pulled out a new envelope, wrote "Space 8" on the front of it with a pen she found on the desk and sealed some cash inside. She had intended to write the date, but when she glanced down at the dive watch on her wrist, it had stopped running. The watch was a graduation gift from her mom. Ava wore it every day, loving the glowing pink numbers encircling its big black face and that it was analog rather than digital. She assumed its quartz battery had died. She glanced around the office for a calendar or a clock with a date featured on it but found nothing. Ava racked her brains, trying to remember today's date. She was sure she'd been thinking about it on the way here, but the information was irretrievable to her now. Eventually, she gave up and added her undated envelope to the stack in the drawer.

By the time the moon had risen over the desert hills, she was freshly showered and eating an apple pie. She wondered what had prompted her to inspect the money in the office trailer. What had she expected to find, Monopoly bills? She couldn't have said, but something struck her as odd about this town, and she wanted to understand it. Still, she liked it here. She wondered about the owners of the vintage Airstream, which was spick and span and suited her to a T. She saw nothing inside that could tell her about the women or where they had gone on their "indefinite holiday." What was an indefinite holiday, anyway? Surely, a person either was or was not on holiday. Maybe Jack had meant that their return was indefinite? Probably that, Ava decided.

The day had come good in the end, she thought. Good food, a hot shower, and shampoo that smelled like orange blossoms had lifted her spirits. She used her fingers to comb out her wet hair, which she'd cropped short with kindergarten scissors just last week. They'd been the cheapest pair available at the drugstore, and she'd been frustrated with the long tangled mess her hair had become. The past few nights, she'd had to wash as best she could in public bathrooms and sleep rough in parks.

She was not homeless, at least not permanently. Once she got back to L.A., her mother would be happy to have her home, where she could keep an eye on her. Ava would not tell her about the many nights she'd slept outdoors during her travels, unable to scrape together enough cash for a room. She knew that Jeannie would have worried, even though she had been careful to stay out of sight of other people, which had meant tucking herself under bushes, as far away from sidewalks and roads as possible. She would barely sleep those nights, and there had been a string of them this past week. She'd been desperate for a room tonight.

Ava had traveled through a dozen Southern states during the past two years and enjoyed a good run until recently, but piecemeal work was getting harder to come by due to the economy taking a downturn and the media forecasting doom and gloom for the nation. Ava didn't listen to the news often, but there was usually a radio or TV on wherever she stopped to eat so she couldn't help but hear some of it. She knew she could have called Jeannie, who would have scraped together whatever money she had and sent it to her, but she didn't want to be rescued. Still, she'd known it was time to call an end to her journey when she'd put on her tightest jeans and felt them slide down past her hip bones. Enough was enough.

People are hard work, she thought, as she considered the lovely-looking but antagonistic Jasmine. She was appreciative tonight, though, for the help she'd received from strangers and glad to have finally come up with a third item for this evening's gratitude list: this cozy camper. Thinking of this, she pulled out her notebook and began to write.

It was a non-negotiable rule for Ava that the number of items on her list had to be divisible by three. Though not religious, she organized her life around private rituals and acts of devotion. There were many trinities in her world, all of them holy. In her pack or pocket, she carried an advisory committee of laminated saints, the three Marys, which she consulted regularly on matters of importance. She considered her daily journaling to be her most disciplined ritual and had never missed an entry except for times of illness.

She enjoyed writing to other people, too, even though the words in her head rarely came out the way she intended. She did this the old-fashioned way, writing longhand in pencil or ink, and sending letters through the post. An outlier in her generation, she avoided computers as much as possible and kept an electric typewriter at home for formal occasions. Ava had never owned a mobile phone or an MP3 player. Video games and virtual worlds were had failed to capture her interest. Her unwillingness to use these quotidian technologies had alienated her classmates, who had written her off as socially dead.

Jeannie had given her a set of a dozen colorful, pocket-sized notebooks, fitted into a black slipcase, which Ava kept in a waterproof compartment at the bottom of her travel pack, along with her bird books. She'd used these sparingly, allocating loose stationery for letters and saving her notebooks for daily journaling, lists, and sketches. Even so, she had only one notebook left, which was the blazing orange of a flame-colored tanager.

She unzipped her pack to retrieve her notebooks and papers, having decided to complete her evening reflections first and then write to Jeannie, to let her know where she was and when she would be home. Jeannie had not insisted on letters but asked only that Ava call and drop her a postcard from time to time. Nevertheless, Ava wrote to her weekly too. Her letters home began predictably with "Dear Mom" and ended with "Love, Ava," but between the openings and closings were usually lists and pencil or ink sketches, rather than narratives: the towns she'd visited, their local flora and fauna, what she'd eaten, and any quirky landmarks she thought Jeannie might like. Lists, Ava believed, were the best use of her words. They were clear and orderly and said what she meant them to say.

She felt a stab of guilt as she began writing, remembering Jeannie's worrying over her traveling alone. Despite her concern, Jeannie had accepted Ava's decision and taken her shopping for her trip. She was a good mom, Ava thought, although they'd had their moments of frustration with each other over the years. Jeannie was a highly emotional woman, and Ava found her impossible to understand at times. Ava herself was not prone to expressing her feelings much, as people were forever pointing out to her, like it was a bad thing.

As she sorted through her writing implements, she realized how happy she felt, which surprised her because it had been a while since "happy" had appeared in her personal vocabulary. She did not think of herself as hard to please because her emotional palette was uncluttered and her needs straightforward. Mostly, she liked to be left alone to study birds and plants and to wander through the natural world as an appreciative explorer. She preferred order over chaos, silence over noise, and paths of least resistance. During her final year of school, she had also preferred Bobbie Jo Slater over everyone else. Nevertheless, BJ had broken off their relationship, dismissing any impact this would have on "whatever passes for your heart, Ava." That's what BJ had said, the last time Ava had seen her. Ava dismissed BJ from her mind and opened the orange notebook. She wrote:

> *Earlier this evening, I was grateful for having some money, and for warmth instead of cold, and for no third thing I could think of, but now I know: the truck driver who brought me here, to this stranger place than any I have known. Now that I am here, I am grateful too for the man at the grocery store who told me I could stay, for this camper with the delicious pie, and for feeling like I am . . ."*

Again, she surprised herself, but the only word that came to mind was the one she wrote down in bold capital letters:

HOME.

Two

Ava sat in a booth that allowed her a view out the front door of the Flying Saucer Diner so she could keep an eye on her bag of recyclables. Opening her eyes this morning, she'd felt excited to be here, wherever *here* was, and she'd noticed a mild vibration throughout her body, like a live current. She'd been stretching out her tingling muscles when she'd spotted a coupon on the floor, beneath the door's mail slot. It was the size of an index card, printed in purple ink on white paper, with a peculiar odor that she'd sniffed three times, twice lightly and once deeply. It lacked an aura of authority, so she half expected it to be declined by the waitress, especially since the waitress turned out to be Jasmine from the grocery store. Ava watched the young woman sauntering to her table and wondered how she might make a fresh start with her after last night's snit, but the waitress either did not recognize her or had decided to pretend they'd never met. Ava looked at the girl's badge and read, "Hi, I'm Julie!"

Glancing briefly at the coupon, Julie met Ava's gaze directly and asked, "What'll you have?"

Ava ordered her meal while pondering the waitress's name tag. Were Jasmine and Julie twins, or was "Julie" her waitress name and "Jasmine" her grocery-clerk name? If they were twins, she thought, then they were identical, like clones of each other. Ava sipped coffee and examined her coupon again.

> **This coupon entitles the bearer* to free meals at the Flying Saucer Diner.**
>
> **The bearer* is entitled to a guided tour, upon request.**
>
> **The bearer* may or may not be entitled to a ride on the Infinite Loop, pending our further acquaintance.**
>
> **—M(1a)**
>
> ***Bearer is defined as one who is entitled or invited to hold this coupon.**

The words were cyclical and silly but apparently valid because Julie slid a plate of hot food in front of her in no time and walked away without further comment. Ava nibbled her toast and wondered about the Infinite Loop. She'd seen a couple of signs for it already, one on a sandwich board right next to the grocery store, and one in the RV park, painted in white letters on a red brick wall. These advertisements reminded her of road trips with her mom. Inevitably, the two of them would follow billboards to towns they had not planned to visit, simply to assuage their curiosity about the world's largest ball of lint or most complex hedge maze. Usually, these sites failed to live up to their promised thrills. Ava suspected the Infinite Loop would be an ordinary carnival ride but figured the tour might be worth taking. She decided to ask Julie about it if the waitress would deign to speak to her. Ava smoothed the edges of her coupon and was momentarily at a loss about where to put it until she realized it could form a trio with her notebook and pen.

She examined her surroundings while eating scrambled eggs and toast, pleased to discover that the butter was real, the preserves homemade, and the juice and coffee fresh. This town sure knew a thing or two about food. She'd visited a lot of small and mid-sized towns in the past two years, preferring their slower pace to the hubbub of cities, and had frequently found the food in the affordable diners and cafes either mediocre or just plain bad. The diner was attractive too. Furnished with red vinyl seats, white tables and counter tops, a beautiful jukebox, and a black and white checkerboard linoleum floor, it reminded Ava of the Airstream. Conspicuous by their absence were a TV blaring a morning news show, an untidy rack of papers by the exit, and a gaggle of children hanging over the back of the next booth staring at her.

Three men sat at the counter with their backs to her. They were having pie and coffee and looked to be engrossed in conversation, although she couldn't hear them. Ava observed them leaning toward each other ever so slightly, and thought she could see their mouths moving; but, then again, maybe they were just eating their pie. From her vantage point, the men looked remarkably similar in profile, and the triplet effect was enhanced by their matching gray, lightweight wool suits and black bowler hats. Ava wondered if they were Amish.

She'd finished her breakfast and coffee and was sitting motionless in her booth, smiling to herself, when an idea drifted into her head. She caught the waitress's eye and motioned to her.

"I was wondering about the coupon," she said. "How long can I use it?"

"For however long you have it."

"Seriously?" Ava asked.

Julie gave a shrug. "Sure. Anything else?"

"Yes. Is there anywhere in town that offers refunds on empty cans and bottles?"

The waitress shook her head. "Nope, sorry. We have someone pick up our cans and bottles, but there's no money back for them."

"Thanks for telling me. It saves me lugging my bag around looking for a buy-back center." Ava pointed to a line on her coupon and asked, "My coupon mentions a guided tour. Do you know where I should go for that?"

"That I do know. Check back here later today or tomorrow. One of our guides will be around then. It's an informal arrangement; you don't need an appointment."

"Thanks." Ava decided to test her theory about Jasmine and Julie being the same person, so she asked, "There's just one more thing if you don't mind? I want to get in touch with the man last night who helped me at the grocery store, the one you called Jack. Do you know how I can find him?"

The waitress's head twitched, dropping a thick dark curl across her right eye. She stared at Ava and puckered her lips as if she were sucking a lemon drop. The bright green eyes narrowed in the confines of her thick black liner.

"That wasn't me," she said. After a silence in which the sour gaze lingered, she added, "There's only one Jack in town, and he and his wife, Annie, own Cafe Z. You can usually find them there, but they're busy cooking most of the time. They've recently extended their hours, which means they're open from lunchtime till whenever Jack decides to lock the doors. Besides that, they're the caterers of choice for the visitor center. Good luck catching him."

Ava felt her face flush. She could've sworn this was the same girl she'd met last night. Her voice even held the same husky timbre as Jasmine's, which had surprised Ava. She'd not thought much about it at the time, given her exhaustion and defensiveness, but she had thought about it later. It was a sultry voice, where she'd been expecting a soprano. Despite Jasmine's rudeness, Ava had to admit that she had liked her. In fact, she'd liked her quite a lot, she now realized, because she was disappointed that this was not Jasmine.

The waitress had the same face, the same hair, and the same body as Jasmine. She wore the same white cotton blouse, plain blue jeans, and red polka-dot scarf. If Jasmine had worn red tennis shoes with white laces, the two would match perfectly. Ava had not seen Jasmine's feet behind the grocery store counter but imagined they would have been as small as Julie's, with her shoes chosen to complement her outfit. She decided the two must be twins but then wondered why Julie did not say, "That's my sister." Why the scowly face?

Not waiting for Ava to respond, Julie turned her back and walked away, her hips swaying like the femme fatale's in an old movie. In fact, everything about her suggested film noir: sexy, edgy, a bit mean, and probably dangerous. *Just like Jasmine, but not.* An important difference between the two, as far as Ava was concerned, was that only thoughts of Jasmine produced butterflies.

As Ava was leaving, she thought one of the men at the counter moved; but, when she turned to look, all three were staring down at their pie. She collected her recycling bag at the door and headed back to the camper, having settled on staying in town a while longer. Jack had said that she was welcome to the Airstream, and he hadn't said only one night.

Since she had free food and lodging, there was no need to rush off.

Ava wondered why she had been offered these gifts, but presumed she would find out soon enough. Maybe it was just a brand of desert hospitality, unique to this place. Nevertheless, she'd need some money to get home to L.A., or else she'd have to hitch rides again. If she stayed in town for a week and picked up odd jobs, she could earn enough money for a bus or train ticket.

She stopped back by the camper to drop off her recycling bag and to unzip her small day pack from the front of her travel pack. She felt much lighter with only the day pack on her back, and half skipped as she headed off for a stroll around town. As she made her way through the RV park, she noticed a swimming pool near the shower block, just as Jack had said there would be, though she hadn't seen it last night.

Ava looked for the town's name on all the shop fronts she passed but failed to find it. She still had no idea where she was and felt unsure about asking, as if it should have been obvious to her by now. Since Jasmine had made it clear that it wasn't California, maybe it was a nearby state, like Arizona or Nevada. She'd been heading west when the trucker had picked her up . . . Where? Where had she been when they met? Oklahoma? Texas? Ava couldn't recall, but she decided to worry about that later.

She was distracted by all the places dotted around town which she couldn't remember seeing yesterday. It was as if they'd popped up out of nowhere, where only empty blocks of land had been before. It hadn't been very late when she'd walked into town and stopped at the grocery store, which was the first place she'd reached on the main street. It was true that she hadn't walked farther than the RV park last night, but it seemed likely that she would have seen the shops a few blocks down and across from where she was staying. She could have sworn there'd been only a grass lot where now there were a drugstore, a record shop, and a revival-house cinema. Beyond the cinema was a motel with a "No Vacancy" sandwich board perched on the sidewalk. Glancing across the street from the motel, she was surprised to find a church. *How could I have missed that bell tower?* Ava prided herself on being a quick study of wherever she landed in her travels. It was not like her to overlook even a swimming pool, let alone half a town, in a place this small. And yet, she realized, she must have done just that. She decided to blame yesterday's exhaustion and leave it at that.

After covering one side of the street, she began to think that finding a mailbox might be harder than she'd imagined. She'd seen no post office. She stuffed her letter into the pocket of her jeans and crossed the street to a long, narrow park next to the drugstore. There was a sky-blue sign on the sidewalk featuring a smiling yellow sun and puffy clouds at the top, with grass and flowers along the bottom, like a child would draw. White letters spelled out "Skylights Park: Enjoy Your Stay!" across the center.

Next to the park, painted on the outer side wall of the drugstore, was another advertisement for the Infinite Loop. Ava noticed that it had a retro look to it, like almost everything else in town. The church was far older than any of the other buildings, and a couple of the shops looked newer by two or three decades, but a 1950s aesthetic prevailed. Most of the architecture was mid-century modern and sparkling fresh, as if the town had gone to some trouble to preserve it in its original state. It occurred to Ava that the buildings might have been erected all at once. That would explain why most of them seemed to go together, like a play set with all the pieces matching.

As she entered the park, she noticed with pleasure that it had been landscaped with native mesquite and juniper trees, desert grasses, agave, and yucca. At the back of the park was its grandest feature: a stand of towering ghost gums keeping watch over the land. Ava knew these trees from her local park back home and knew that they had been brought in from Australia, originally, where they appeared in Indigenous Dreamtime myths. She was glad to see them looking alive and well here.

Feeling watched, Ava turned back toward the entrance where, to her delight, she saw an extraordinarily large black-tailed jackrabbit. It sat near the boulders which formed an open gateway to the grounds and appeared to be watching her. Its ears were erect and its nose twitched. It did not run away as Ava approached, so she supposed it was someone's pet, but a quick look around told her the park was empty except for the two of them. Ava crouched down and put out her right hand, palm up. The hare looked at the palm and sniffed, wondering whether food might be there. Smelling nothing edible, it thumped one of its back feet twice, and Ava expected it to hop away. Instead, the jackrabbit moved closer to her and sat very still.

"What is it?" Ava asked.

The hare remained still.

Ava stayed in her crouching position and studied the hare quietly until it occurred to her what it was trying to communicate. Right before her eyes, hanging from a loose cord around the jackrabbit's neck, was a small leather carrying pouch with a top flap to secure its contents.

"Oh, my goodness! Are you a messenger hare?" Ava asked.

The hare stood up on his back legs, as steady and straight as an exclamation point.

Ava reached for the pouch slowly and opened its flap, revealing the edge of a cream-colored envelope. Once she'd pulled the envelope free, she saw that it was roughly the size and shape of a playing card and that it had her name scrawled across the front in black ink.

Ava laughed and reached out to pet the jackrabbit, but it bounded off in the direction of the RV park before she could make contact. She examined the smooth envelope and the red wax seal on its back. The emblem on the seal was a sacred symbol: three hares chasing one another in a circle. While each hare appeared to have two ears, there were only three ears in total, each shared by two of the hares. Ava knew this ancient motif could be found at holy sites around the world and that its meaning was obscure, with interpretations varying from culture to culture.

Around her neck, she wore a silver chain and a pendant that was nearly identical to the image on the wax. Her mother had given it to her for Christmas the year she turned seven, and Ava rarely removed it. The envelope's seal differed in only one crucial respect from her pendant: the hares pressed in wax appeared to be chasing each other around the perimeter of a piecrust.

Ava wondered who could have sent her a message. She'd spoken to only three people since her arrival: Jasmine and Jack at the grocery store and Julie at the diner. She couldn't recall telling any of them her name. Nevertheless, Ava did what anyone would do when delivered a mysterious letter by a messenger hare: she cracked the seal and slid out the paper inside, feeling a tingle up the back of her neck as she did so. The paper was creamy white and as elegant as the envelope. Ava caressed it and then sniffed it several times, before opening it to read. It smelled mildly of pie. Pecan pie, or walnut maybe? Ava wasn't sure since she favored fruit and custard ones herself.

Three

Ava approached the front entrance of the motel and stopped for a moment to stare at the neon sign above the door, which announced that there was "No Vacancy" in the place where one would have expected to see the motel's name. She thought the sandwich board on the sidewalk, which carried the same message, should have been sufficient to get the point across.

She ignored the front doors to the main lobby and dodged left to walk through the motor court's trellised archway, where she passed another entrance with an ice machine next to it before entering the central courtyard. It was a classic roadside motel, built in Spanish colonial revival style, centered around a recreation area featuring lush gardens and an inviting swimming pool. The exteriors of the buildings were white stucco and the roofs burnt-orange tiles. The main building was two stories high and curved, so that its back formed a semicircle on one side of the courtyard, while six free-standing bungalows on the courtyard's opposite side completed the circle. The trees around the pool's fence were a type of eucalyptus Ava recognized as lemon-scented gum. There were some trees like this too at her local park back home. She loved to crush the leaves to release the heady scent of their oils.

The buildings, the pool, and the lilies flourishing beneath the eucalypts all shone bright white in the sunshine. Ava shaded her eyes to study the pool, which she considered unusual. It was perfectly round and appeared deep in the middle, with the shallows circling all the way around. There were white and aqua loungers and a white, wrought-iron fence surrounding it. She opened the gate and let herself in while considering the whole layout.

"Circles in circles," Ava murmured.

"You're right about that," responded a voice behind her.

Ava started and turned. The girl who faced her looked to be about the same height and build as herself: slight but gently curved and a bit taller than average. She was wearing a black bikini, with an unbuttoned denim shirt over it. A straw fedora and oversized sunglasses obscured much of her face. Her lips, which curved into a smile, were the same red as her fingernails and toenails. Her hair was short, like Ava's, but the bits that stuck out beneath her hat shone the familiar gold of California sunshine. Ava couldn't help but notice the similarities between this stranger and the healthier version of herself she'd been before she left L.A. She felt self-consciously ragged by comparison.

"I thought you'd wear a swimsuit," the girl said.

Ava stared blankly at her.

"The note said to meet me at the pool, remember?"

Ava nodded. There had been no signature and no explanation, other than how to find the motel pool, but it hadn't occurred to her she'd been invited to swim.

"No matter. If you want to swim, you can borrow one of mine. It's all the same, isn't it? Anyway, I want to show you around first."

The girl linked her right arm through Ava's left arm and led her through the back door of the main building and behind the service desk of the motel's lobby. Ava's hostess explained that office supplies and fresh coffee were usually available there, and Ava was welcome to help herself.

"Feel free to use the pool or any of our facilities whenever you like," she added.

"What's this place called?" Ava asked.

"It's the No Vacancy Motel," her hostess answered.

"Seriously?"

"Yes, of course. Didn't you see our neon 'No Vacancy' sign? It's hard to miss."

"Yes, but I thought . . ." Ava decided not to continue this line of conversation, as naming a motel "No Vacancy" was certainly not the most peculiar thing she'd come across in this town. "Do you work here?" she asked.

"No. There is no staff. The motel provides long-term housing for local people. We look after our rooms and take turns keeping the public areas clean."

"So, you live here?"

"Me and a few others, yes."

Ava's comment about that being a strange way to run a business was brushed off with the wave of a hand. The girl walked through a doorway across the lobby, her bare feet slapping lightly on the tiled floor. Ava followed her into an airy lounge decorated with walnut paneling, a wall-to-wall cream and gold carpet, burnt orange armchairs, teal sofas, and glass-topped coffee tables. It was the sort of room where you'd find a TV in most motels, but Ava didn't see one. On the wall where she would have expected it, there was instead a large, framed photograph of two young women, one blonde and one brunette and both beautiful, she thought. Next to this one was another photo of—Ava peered closer—the same two women, older by a couple of decades and still attractive. In both shots, the women were smiling at the camera, faces lit with unguarded happiness. Looking at it, Ava felt something she couldn't express, a lightening in her chest. She turned to ask who they were but stopped when she saw the girl touching her fingertips first to her chest and then to the picture on the left and then back to her chest again. It was

25

such an obviously reverent movement that Ava felt that she should bow her head.

The girl's smile broadened. "Our founding mothers," she said. Ava leaned in to get a look at the framed set of drawings hanging beneath the two photographs and discovered that they made up a series of quirky hand-drawn maps. She noticed that the series became more visually complicated as it went along, and appeared to represent the town itself. Ava could see the diner, the RV park, and the gas station with their funny space names penciled on rectangular signs. She scanned the set of drawings again, looking for the name of the town, but found nothing. She turned to ask her hostess about this, but the young woman had left the lounge. Ava found her waiting at the entrance to a hallway leading off the lobby.

"I will tell you more about our founders and our town later," the hostess said.

The motel looked empty, and there were no cars in the parking lot. Ava thought that perhaps the others were at work but wondered where that would be. As they wound their way through the hallways of the first and second floors, her hostess pointed out which were the most and least desirable rooms of the two dozen in the main building. She explained that there were also six one- and two-bedroom bungalows. "The few of us who live here permanently stay in the bungalows, so no one is living in this building, but we look after it just the same."

The young woman then spent several minutes commenting on the "rather good" carpeting in the rooms and the "rather terrible" paintings that hung over the beds and sofas. "But then, I must admit, I've never been one for abstract art."

Ava remained silent, unsure what she was meant to do with this information. She knew little about art, but she could see that the motel's guest rooms had been decorated to harmonize with its public spaces: a style she associated with all-American road trips, circa 1955. California kept this vibe alive, too, but the difference here was that everything looked fresh out of the box.

Ava had many questions that she didn't feel comfortable asking yet, and she couldn't have said why that was the case, except that feeling uncomfortable with people was her typical life experience. There was something different about this girl, though: she seemed nervous too. In fact, she was one of the few people Ava had met in her travels who seemed as socially reticent and conversationally off-key as herself. Ava thought she recognized her own struggle in the young woman's speech pattern and physical mannerisms, both of which halted and then rushed ahead, as if unable to maintain an even pace. She seemed not to know what to do with her body in relation to Ava's. Ava watched the girl adjust and readjust the space between them as they walked and stood near one another. *This is fascinating,* thought Ava, *and kind of tragic.* Despite their unfortunate awkward similarities, Ava had to admit that her hostess's Southern lilt and gentle demeanor were charming.

Eventually, they ended up back at the pool.

"The one with the potted tangerine tree in front of it is mine," the girl said, gesturing toward the bungalows.

"Nice choice."

"Yes. Tangerines are delicious, and we've always liked that color, haven't we?"

"We have?" Ava did like that color but was uncertain about the collective pronoun. She wondered why this stranger was speaking to her as though they'd known each other all their lives. It was true, though, that there was something familiar about her. Had they met before in some forgotten place, at some forgotten time?

Unable to contain herself any longer, Ava blurted out, "Who are you?"

The girl laughed and pulled off her sunglasses with one hand and her hat with the other, mussing her short blonde hair in the process. Ava found herself staring at her own laughing face, or what used to be her face. That was when she'd been still at home, well fed and fussed over by her mom before she'd set off to wander like a vagabond through the back roads of America. Ava glanced down at the girl's chest to see a replica of her own three-hares pendant dangling on a matching silver chain. She gasped and stepped backward several feet and would have fallen into the pool if her hostess had not caught her arm.

"It's okay, Ava. Please don't be frightened."

Ava shook her head and took a deep breath, finding her voice. "Who are you?" she asked again. "What is this place? Are you playing a trick on me?"

"Here, it's better if you sit down. You're trembling." The young woman led Ava to a white lounger and pushed her gently down onto the seat. "I am going to get you a glass of orange juice from my room. I won't be a minute. Please don't leave."

Ava could not have left, even if she'd wanted to. She perched rigidly at the end of the lounger, stunned, and feeling as if the wind had been knocked out of her. Before she could get her thoughts straight, her lookalike was back at her side carrying frothy juice in chilled glasses, with sprigs of mint and striped straws poking out of the top. Ava took a glass and drank it half down, getting a brain freeze as she did so. She put her head down and pinched her nose to make it stop, then sat staring at her better-looking mirror image, waiting for her to speak.

The girl sat next to Ava on the white lounger. "I am Evelyn," she explained. "This place is Pie Town, and we are in no way playing a trick on you. Having said that, as our birthday is in a few days, I can't promise there won't be more surprises coming your way." Evelyn smiled, but Ava edged away from her as far as she could without falling off the lounger.

"*Our* birthday? It is *my* birthday. I'll turn twenty-one on Friday. What day is today, anyway? I keep losing track of things."

Evelyn did not respond immediately. Ava plucked up her courage and took a long, hard look at the girl before asking quietly, "Are you telling me that, besides looking like twins, we share the same birthday?"

The young woman maintained her silence, as though waiting for Ava to reach her own conclusions. Eventually, Ava did. "I'm sure I've never met you in my life," she said, but even as the words left her mouth, she felt a gnawing uncertainty. There was something here that felt deeply personal, but it was not about looks. It was subtler than that.

Evelyn laughed lightly and stood up from the lounger so quickly that Ava nearly toppled off the end. "Well, it's no surprise that you don't remember, Ava," she said.

She began to pace and gesticulate as she spoke, making Ava feel that she was watching a performance rather than having a conversation.

"Nevertheless, I am something like a twin to you. Let's say I'm like a sister you never knew you had or one you don't remember having. Happily, we do share a birthday, and I'm looking forward to spending it with you and our other friends. I wouldn't be too concerned with trifles like days of the week, but today is something like a Tuesday, give or take." She paused in her pacing and faced Ava directly, giving her words time to sink in.

It was Ava's turn to jump up from the lounger and pace, which she did not normally do. "'Something like a twin'? 'Something like a Tuesday'? What are you talking about, Evelyn? That sounds completely crazy."

Suddenly, Evelyn reached out and stopped Ava by grasping her upper arms and peering into her eyes. "Hey, how about we have some lunch? You can take a quick swim while I whip up sandwiches. I make terrific club sandwiches, Ava, with fancy cheese and olives skewered on frilly toothpicks, the whole shebang. You'll be glad you came once we've had lunch. I promise."

Ava stared at Evelyn, who was beaming at her as if she'd just won a prize at the county fair. She realized then that Evelyn's speech and movements had begun to seem more natural and confident ever since they'd started their birthday discussion. Her Southern accent flowed as sweet and easy as warm maple syrup over buttermilk pancakes.

"As you know, I didn't bring a swimsuit," Ava answered. Unlike Evelyn, she did not feel any more at ease than she had five minutes ago.

"Not a problem. I think we're about the same size." Evelyn laughed at her own joke, while Ava stared at her, unresponsive, and mesmerized by the truth of that statement. Yes. They were very close to the same size, with Evelyn the size Ava would be if she hadn't dropped weight over the past few months. They were the same everything, judging by appearance. They even sounded alike, except for regional differences. Ava sounded like a California girl and Evelyn like a Georgia peach, but the timbre and cadence of their soprano voices were otherwise indistinguishable.

Ava tried to think of three calm things as she followed Evelyn to the room with the tangerine tree outside. Remembering the serene Marys resting in her jeans pocket, she ran her fingers over their laminated faces and murmured a prayer under her breath.

Evelyn pulled out a black bikini, identical to the one she had on, and handed it to Ava. Ava changed in the bathroom but avoided looking in the mirror. When she came out, she found Evelyn preparing lunch.

"A bit warm in here, isn't it? A swim will be just the thing," Evelyn said.

Ava didn't reply, but she hadn't felt too hot or too cold at any time since arriving in Pie Town. She was chronically tingly and frequently confused but, thermally speaking, she felt fine. In fact, the weather was perfect: sunny and clear to partly cloudy, with an occasional gentle breeze, like the best days in Southern California. Nights were cool, but not cold.

Evelyn pulled off her denim shirt to reveal a silvery-pink birthmark, a shimmering oval just beneath her lowest left rib. Ava stared at it but did not flinch. Given their other similarities, she had half expected it. Silently, she extended her right index finger to rub the imperfect oval with the smudgy edges. Evelyn stood still, allowing the contact, as Ava confirmed for herself that the mark was indelible. Just like her own. *Dead ringers, like Jasmine and Julie,* she thought, but she kept her silence. She asked no more questions, and Evelyn offered no further explanations.

Moments later, Ava was standing next to the round pool, feeling inexplicably calm and light as air. She considered the possibility that her orange juice had been spiked with a tranquilizer, but it was also possible the Marys had done their job. Whatever the cause, she felt better, and that was what mattered. She slipped into the pool, enjoying the lapping of cool water against her skin.

After half a dozen laps, she dived deeper, and then deeper still when she realized that she could not make out the bottom of the pool. Before entering, she'd contemplated the concentric rings which formed a stairway toward its center and had estimated its depth as no more than twelve to fifteen feet. As she plunged downward, she could see where the bottom should have been, but it appeared to be a black hole rather than a solid surface.

"At the still point, there the dance is," drifted through Ava's mind, in her mother's voice. It was a favorite quote of Jeannie's, who had studied poetry at college and favored the works of T.S. Eliot. Ava didn't know why she thought of it now. Rather than being still, the center of the pool seemed to recede farther into the distance as she descended. This was disorienting, but she didn't panic. She had an exceptional talent for holding her breath, a skill which she had been practicing since childhood. She was confident she could last five minutes underwater, but with a dead dive watch, it would be hard to know when to begin surfacing. She thought she spotted a breathing dome near the black hole, which now appeared closer than the surface. Ava gave a strong dolphin kick and thrust downward.

Four

She is three years old, and she's wearing her hot pink Dora the Explorer swimsuit. Her mother has brought her to the beach to get a start on teaching her to swim in the ocean. She's already explained that this is different from the swimming pool at the YMCA, and far more dangerous, so the child isn't listening to the repeat version that accompanies her mother's pulling on her swim cap. She isn't splashing in the surf or looking for shells, either, like other children would have done. Instead, she is standing stock-still in the shallows, staring out to sea.

Jeannie says something about not removing her floaties, at least this first time. The child doesn't care. At this moment, all she wants in the whole world is for the two of them to rush headlong into the waves and dog-paddle to the horizon together. They will dangle their legs over the edge of the earth and sing songs until their throats go hoarse. They will sprout feathers and wings and soar into the soft blue sky. As she imagines this, she waves her arms at her sides in a flapping motion and looks for words to explain all that she is feeling. "Like the birds, Mama, like the birds. But first, like the fish. We have to swim all the way to there first."

Jeannie looks to "there" and says, "You want to swim all the way to the horizon, as far as you can see?"

The child claps her hands and laughs. "Yes!" she says. "Yes! All the way!"

She is not a child who laughs easily or often, so Jeannie hesitates before kneeling in the surf to bring them eye level with each other. She does not offer a second-best option because she knows her girl well enough to know that never works. She tells her the truth instead. Jeannie explains that although the horizon looks not so far away, it is like rainbows and sunsets: "We can never reach it, darling, no matter how fast we swim or what distances we cover."

The child bursts into tears and reaches out to stroke her mother's face, a self-soothing gesture that calms her in times of distress. Jeannie laughs gently and pulls her into her arms, hugging her close, competing with the strength of the waves.

"It's getting late, anyway. Mommy has left it too late. Let's go get ice cream for dinner and come back here on another day, earlier, when we might at least get a start on the horizon."

"Okay, Mama," she answers. Her desolation is too big for her, so she says nothing else. She can feel her orange floaties constricting her arms, up past her elbows. She tastes the saltwater that has splashed her face and feels a gentle wind already drying the bits of her that are above the waves.

Jeannie crouches low to get a better grip and then lifts her clear of the water, except for her toes. "Cheer up, buttercup, or we'll have to let the fish nibble your toes," Jeannie says, and the girl giggles despite her sadness because she doesn't want her mother feeling sad too. Besides, she thinks, ice cream for dinner is a good end to the day.

Five

"Ava! Ava! Ava! Ava! Ava! Ava!"

Ava rocketed up to the surface of the water and emerged gasping for air.

Evelyn was standing at the edge of the pool, holding a tray piled high with food and repeating Ava's name like a panicky mantra. Ava swam to the shallows and stepped up onto the concrete pod, where she watched as Evelyn set the lunch tray on a table between two of the loungers. Evelyn turned to Ava with her arms flung wide, and her palms turned upward to the sky as though playing to an audience only she could see. Ava thought this a dramatic gesture, even for a Southerner. Evelyn's eyes were as wide open and round as the pool, and her brows arched like a Japanese footbridge.

"Hell's bells, Ava, you had me worried there for a minute! Are you okay? You were lying on the bottom of the pool, totally still. I thought you'd drowned!"

"I'm fine," Ava answered, turning away from Evelyn and pulling a towel off the closest lounger. Ava didn't believe her. If Evelyn had thought she'd drowned, wouldn't she would have done more than yell her name hysterically while keeping a death grip on a tray of sandwiches?

"I should have warned you to stay in the shallows, but I had no idea our infinity pool would open itself up like that. It's particular and, under normal circumstances, does not offer communion until it gets to know a person better."

Ava didn't reply. She was not shaken or even a little distressed but thought that maybe she should have been. In fact, she felt deeply relaxed but even less communicative than usual. She had no words for what was going on inside her, for herself or anyone else. Evelyn was subdued during lunch, too, so it was a quieter affair than either had intended.

Ava had that ravenous feeling that typically follows an hour or more of swimming, but she was sure that she'd only been in the pool for a few minutes. Her body felt heavy after the buoyancy of the water. Evelyn said something that Ava didn't catch but, instead of asking her to repeat herself, Ava dismissed her with a shake of her head and they finished their lunch.

After the meal, they reclined in the loungers, still not speaking. A state of repose was beginning to feel natural between the two of them. Evelyn had put her sunglasses on, so Ava couldn't see whether she was asleep or awake, but she had the feeling of being watched. She tried closing her own eyes for a nap and, when that didn't work, she let herself take in the details of the motel. Over and over she felt her gaze drawn back to the pool, but she forced it away to focus on flowers or trees or bungalows.

"When was this motel built?" she asked.

"Either the nineteen nineties or last year. It's hard to say," Evelyn answered.

"That makes no sense."

Evelyn laughed. "You learn to accept that here."

Ava noticed the black-tailed jackrabbit from the park hopping out of the motel's main building on his way to one of the bungalows. The bungalow door opened as the hare approached it, and a muscle-bound guy about Ava's age stepped outside just far enough to tuck an envelope into the messenger's carrier pouch. As the hare hopped off, the young man looked over toward Ava and Evelyn, waved at them, and closed his door.

"Yes," Ava said, "I guess you must."

For a long time, they were quiet again. It was not until Ava moved to the edge of the pool, thinking her companion had dozed off in the sun, that Evelyn spoke up.

"Stop staring at it. You cannot go back in there right now. You are nowhere near ready," Evelyn called to Ava's back, startling her.

She has been watching me the whole time, Ava thought.

Evelyn whipped off her sunglasses and stared directly into Ava's sea-blue eyes with her own sea-blue eyes. "Sorry. I didn't mean to sound harsh. When I invited you for a swim earlier, it never occurred to me that . . . Look, it's too soon. You can't see the bottom of the pool, can you, Ava?"

Ava shook her head. "Not when I'm in the water, no. From here, it appears to be a regular pool."

Her legs dangled in the shallows while her eyes sought the pool's unreachable heart. More than any other strangeness she'd encountered in this place, she found this pool irresistible. She felt like something important had happened in its depths but was unable to remember anything except swimming toward the black hole and then hearing a whisper in her ear seconds before Evelyn began screaming her name.

Ava had to admit to herself that even though the pool didn't feel any more dangerous than her mother's womb, Evelyn probably had saved her life. She'd completely lost track of how long she'd been underwater: dissociation, it was called, like when people were driving on the highway and missed their exit by five miles because they'd stepped outside their brains for a while. Ava didn't drive, but she'd been known to space out from time to time, a habit which worried Jeannie. Just as Evelyn had done, Jeannie would repeat Ava's name like a mantra, calling her home from wherever she'd gone. *But softly, so softly,* Ava thought. Her mother never yelled, except when she was saying goodbye.

Where had she gone this time? Ava continued to stare at the pool whose perfect silence beckoned her. She glanced at Evelyn but did not hold her gaze.

"What I mean to say, Ava, and please forgive me if I am awkward, is that I would like to have all the right words for you, the ones you need and want to hear, but words are not my best thing. I don't use them all that well when it comes to complicated subjects, by which I mean emotional ones, things that matter to people on a personal level. Those things are nearly impossible for me to talk about and get right."

Ava did look at her then. She said, "That's another thing we have in common. Words are hard. I love the way they look on paper and the way they sound, but they are fickle friends and hard to get in the right order when you need them most. They almost never come out how I mean them. People are so sensitive when you get the words wrong, or when you say them at the wrong time, or fail to say them at the right time. People leave when you get the words wrong too often."

Evelyn joined Ava by the pool, slipping her legs in gently so as not to disturb the water too much. "Yes, I find that, too," she said. "That's why it's hard for me to be your hostess, but I have been chosen, and it is right that it should be me. For all practical purposes, I am your next of kin here."

Ava looked hard at Evelyn then, squinting into the sun as she did so. "My mother, Jeannie, is my only next of kin. I don't even know you. Are you trying to tell me that my mother had twins? If that's the case, I don't believe you. And even if it were true, what were the chances we would ever meet?"

"No, that's not how things are, not quite. I know you are confused and feeling impatient. All the same, I think it would be best if we could spend time together and if you would try to trust the process. Let things unfold in their own time, and let the town reveal itself to you on its own terms. The truth is that even if I did my best to answer all of your questions right here and now, you wouldn't half believe me. Other people's words—my words—cannot replace direct experience. There are things you should see for yourself. Seeing is believing, right?"

Ava stared once again into the pool. "I don't know if that is right. Maybe we can be just as easily deceived by what we see as what we hear."

"The pool is not trying to deceive you. It is simply being itself. I would never have told you to take a swim had I realized you would not see the bottom. Usually, newcomers here see only an ordinary pool, though, admittedly, one shaped like a crater from a spaceship landing—"

"—Because that's what it is, isn't it?"

"Yes, indeedy, Ava Louise, that's what it is."

Ava laughed, surprising herself. "You know my middle name too. I guess I shouldn't be surprised."

"It's the same as mine. Evelyn Louise, at your service, Ma'am."

"Evelyn Louise? You're joking," Ava replied, feeling her stomach flip-flopping.

"Dead serious, actually." Evelyn smiled and gave Ava a quick peck on the cheek.

Ava blushed and turned away.

"Sorry. I was only trying to make friends. I'm not good at it, obviously."

"No, don't be sorry. It was a kind thing to do. I just haven't been touched much by anyone, let alone kissed, since

I left home two years ago. I've been traveling on my own. Before that, usually, only my mom would kiss me. And for a while, there was someone else." Ava fell silent and began to swirl the pool water with her fingers. "It's like a dream down there, swimming toward that dark center."

Evelyn stood up. "How about we have some pie?" She smiled down at Ava and offered her hand, which Ava took. They wandered back to Evelyn's room together, and while Ava changed out of her swimsuit, Evelyn set a kettle boiling and pulled a fresh pie from the refrigerator. Ava noticed that two settings of plates, cups, and silver had been laid on a wicker table by the window.

"People here sure do eat a lot of pie," Ava said. "I've never been anywhere where pie was a staple food."

"We are famous for it, and we strive to maintain our reputation," Evelyn explained while cutting thick slices of chocolate meringue for the two of them. "People travel crazy distances just to eat our pie. It wouldn't do to disappoint."

"Evelyn, I know this may sound funny, but I thought I was in California when a trucker I'd hitched a ride with dropped me off last night. Now I'm not sure. Is Pie Town in California or not?"

Evelyn licked the pie slicer and a couple of her fingers before passing Ava a plate. She met Ava's eyes with another of her direct, no-nonsense stares. Ava recognized those eyes, but she was sure she did not have that stare. "Ava darlin', this ain't California," Evelyn said.

She'd thickened the Southern accent, which Ava liked both for its lyrical quality and for its being a distinction between them. It occurred to Ava that, although Evelyn's appearance had startled her initially, it was hard to remain adversarial toward someone who looked so much like you. Once the shock wore off, there was an implicit sense of intimacy. If this person looked like her on the outside, did that mean she was like her on the inside too? All Ava knew for certain was that although she was starting to like Evelyn, Evelyn also made her nervous.

Ava caught herself daydreaming and realized Evelyn was still staring at her.

"Sorry, I think I spaced out for a minute there," she explained. "Evelyn, I will try not to bombard you with all my questions at once and to 'trust the process,' as you say, but there are some basic facts I'd like to know now, such as what state we are in since we've established it's not California. Also, is the pool really a crater from a saucer crash or are you teasing me? If you are going to tease me, you need to know that I am as famous for missing punch lines as this town is for its pie." Ava was recalling BJ's habit of cracking jokes all the time, and how offended she'd be when Ava would stare back at her, uncomprehending. It's not that she couldn't tell that BJ was being funny. She could glean that from her general tone and demeanor. She just never got the jokes.

Ava took a seat at the table and was surprised to realize she was hungry again. She dived into the pie while Evelyn poured coffee and watched her eat.

"Those are good questions. Perfectly reasonable. No, I am not teasing you. I am not much of a comedian myself and, when I do say something funny, you will know because I tend to laugh at my own jokes—probably because they are the only ones I get. Like you, other people's humor mostly passes me by.

"Now, the answer to the first question is that we are not in any state or country, technically speaking, but in our own region. In Pie Town, it is customary to refer to anywhere that shares our planet but exists outside our borders as the 'outer desert.' In your geographical terms, you arrived via the

Chihuahuan Desert, which spreads across parts of West Texas, New Mexico, and Arizona on the U.S. side. There are other ways one can end up here, but that's another story. Anyway, you walked a bit from where you were dropped off, right?"

"Yes, how'd you know?" Ava thought back to yesterday afternoon, which seemed forever ago. Suddenly, she could recall the hours she'd spent riding and talking with the trucker, including how surprised he had looked when she'd asked to be let out.

Six

His name was Burke, and Ava liked him. He'd picked her up in El Paso at a diner where they'd both been ordering coffee to go. He'd let her ride with him all day and even offered to buy her lunch, but Ava demurred, sharing only his thermos of coffee when hers ran out. She hadn't wanted to feel indebted, and anything beyond a ride would have felt like that. Burke told her about his life, while she told him her name and not much else. He hadn't seemed to mind or perhaps hadn't noticed. Burke talked about his family and said his youngest daughter was sixteen and he'd ground her for the rest of her life if he ever caught her taking rides from strangers. He did not approve of young women traveling on their own, and especially not hitchhiking. He'd refrained from lecturing her until near dusk when Ava woke suddenly from her nap and, without preamble, insisted that he stop the truck because she had to get out *now*. She'd startled Burke, who'd thought she was dead asleep.

"Here? Why here, girl? There's nothing but desert for a hundred miles in any direction. Where you think you're gonna go?"

"Yes, here," Ava insisted, hanging her head out the window like a golden retriever. She scanned the horizon for a town that she knew must be there because it was calling her name. At least, that's what had happened in the dream she'd been having, but she didn't want to tell Burke that. He'd think she was nuts. Besides, she couldn't remember anything else about the dream except the beckoning.

"I want to collect some of those cans to add to the few I've got here, and then I'll walk to that town over there." She pointed off the highway, to the right. "It can't be more than a few miles, and I can look for more recyclables on the way."

"What are you talking about? We are hell and gone from any town, Ava."

Maybe it was too small to be a proper town; from this distance, Ava couldn't tell. Nevertheless, she was getting out and walking to it regardless of Burke's approval.

"Look, Burke, I appreciate the ride and the coffee and conversation. You've been great. And thanks for letting me sleep too. I needed that. If you just let me out here, I'll be fine. I've changed my plans and decided to extend my trip for another couple of days."

Realizing he couldn't keep her there, Burke had changed tack. "Do you have a phone?"

"No, I don't carry one. Why?"

"What if you get into trouble?" Burke was fishing around under his seat, and Ava watched as he pulled out a socket wrench, a pile of old maps, half a wrapped sandwich, a bottle of Coke, and a bundled-up t-shirt covered in motor oil. Burke unbundled the shirt and pulled out a cell phone, passing it to her. "You take this."

Ava hesitated.

"If you don't take this phone, then I will kidnap you until we get to a decent town, where I will unkidnap you and set you free. And I'll still make you take a phone with you after all that. This one here is a backup phone. I always carry a couple of pre-paid ones with me because I have a habit of losing the damn things."

Ava sighed and took the phone.

"The first number in there is for my regular phone. Sometimes, I lose it in the truck and find it by calling the number on that one." Burke smiled at her, clearly relieved she'd accepted his gift. "You call me if you get on up the road and don't find what you're looking for. I understand you might want to hitch another ride. You might be tired of me lecturing you by now, and that's okay. I been like this ever since my kids came along and can't seem to stop myself."

Ava smiled, wanting to be kind but impatient to be on her way.

"You give me a call if no one comes by after a while, you hear? I'll come back for you. And if I can't, I'll call a friend on this route to pick you up. You take care now, Ava."

Seven

She remembered shaking Burke's extended hand absently, as she had stopped listening by then, focusing instead on gathering her things and moving on. His words rushed back to her now, in full. He'd thought she wanted out to wait for another ride because she was tired of being with him. He hadn't believed that she'd just wanted to collect the cans she could see out the window and then walk to the town she'd pointed to, a few miles off the main highway.

He didn't believe me because he didn't see any town.

Ava set down her fork and swallowed hard. She glanced up at Evelyn, who sat perfectly still, watching her. Evelyn's coffee and pie were untouched and her gaze serene.

"Evelyn?"

"Yes, Ava?"

"You haven't answered my second question, about the pool." Ava's voice sounded so soft and vulnerable that she almost regretted speaking.

"Yes, Ava, that's true. I am thinking about that. I am going to try to get this right, but please tell me if I upset you because you cannot rely on me to notice. I don't always. Or so I am told. Repeatedly. I don't always notice when I've caused a disturbance."

"I understand because I'm the same way, but I think it's obvious that I am already disturbed. Please, tell me whatever you can about the pool and the town and indefinite holidays and you and me and delivery hares." Ava gulped half a cup of black coffee and sat up straight, preparing to focus entirely on whatever Evelyn might reveal.

"Hare," Evelyn replied.

"What?" Ava asked.

"Hare," she repeated. "There's only the one. We call him Harvey because of that old Jimmy Stewart movie. You know *Harvey*? It plays at our cinema. We have a few that we like to see over and over because they are our favorites. Also, we have only a few dozen movies in stock, so our options are limited. Even so, *Harvey* is a favorite-favorite."

"Sure, I know it. My mom and I love that movie," Ava smiled at the memory of curling up with Jeannie and the cats to watch Jimmy Stewart movies. *Harvey* was their favorite too.

Our Harvey is a genuine black-tailed jackrabbit and not a pooka, like the character in the movie. He wandered in from the desert one day and never left. We're not entirely sure how or why he came to live among us. At first, those of us who noticed him suspected he'd crossed our borders by accident, but most of us believe now that the town lured him in."

"*Lured*?" The word sounded sinister to Ava, who had to wonder if she'd been lured too.

"Lured, beckoned . . . Choose whatever word you like, but the fact remains that if Pie Town didn't want Harvey, Harvey wouldn't be here. He used to live in Skylights Park and seemed content there, but then he began to change. For one thing, he grew larger than a regular hare. He's at least three feet high, as you would have noticed, and that's before he stands up on his back feet. But he's changed in other ways too. He's become more like us." Evelyn paused and smiled at Ava. "I guess if you stay here long enough, that's what happens."

Ava considered Evelyn's words and wondered what becoming "more like us" would mean, especially for a hare.

"I'm sure you've noticed that there are precious few animals here at all. It isn't that we don't like them, but they were excluded from the original design—"

"*Design?*" Ava interrupted, self-consciously aware that she was responding to Evelyn's statements by repeating her own words back to her as questions.

"Yes. I'll show you the drawings more closely sometime. Animals were a rather serious oversight, but nobody's perfect. Personally, I'd love a cat. But my first attempt at making one from scratch was not entirely successful, and unless a real one wanders in from the desert for me to copy, it's unlikely future efforts will be any better," Evelyn rambled on, either expecting Ava to understand or not caring that she didn't.

"You tried to make a cat? A *real* cat?" Ava asked.

"Yes ma'am, I certainly did. It was a kind of a hoot, really. Don't worry, though; no animals were harmed in my home experiments. My goal was to recreate Pyewacket from the movie *Bell, Book, and Candle*. You know that one?"

Ava nodded at Evelyn, not quite believing this conversation. "You are telling me that you tried to make a Siamese cat?"

"*Cats*, plural. I was hoping for more than one. Long story short, my pets ended up looking more like plants than cats. Well, that's because they are plants. I tried to turn a variety of climbers and creepers into mammals and ended up with carnivorous vines that yowl when they get hungry and hiss if you irritate them. If you'd like to see them, I can show you. They're planted out back of my bungalow, winding their way up the trellises in my courtyard. I've made a little rock garden back there and even added a pretty fish pond at the center, but I haven't tried making any fish for it yet."

Ava didn't know what to say, so she said nothing. It occurred to her, not for the first time since they'd met, that Evelyn might not be entirely sane.

Evelyn continued. "I don't consider my experiment an utter failure though because I did get the whiskers and ears right and my cat vines are striking: beautiful buff-colored fur with dark chocolate markings. They're pure carnivores, with teeth lining their leafy mouths and claws instead of thorns. Their favorite foods are mackerels and sardines, which I get at the grocery store. I don't stick my fingers too close to them because I'm not sure what else they might like the taste of. I wear thick gloves when I groom them. Would you like to see them? I can't introduce you, unfortunately, because they'll be dead asleep this time of day."

She was looking at Ava, expectantly. Ava wondered if her own eyes ever looked so huge and guileless. And slightly crazy.

Ava cleared her throat. "Uh, that sounds great, but maybe later? I'm a little tired from the swimming, and I'd like to hear more about Harvey and the pool and the town."

"Oh, right!" Evelyn crackled with an energy that was palpable.

The differences between them became more obvious to Ava the longer they were together. Evelyn's facial expressions, especially her smile, were very much her own, as were her mannerisms. She seemed to Ava livelier and more vigorous than herself. If they were birds, Ava thought, Evelyn would be a colorful songbird, and she would be a soft-gray mourning dove.

"Anyhoo, back to Harvey. To make a long hare short— *Ha! Ha!*—" Evelyn interrupted herself. Ava was startled to hear *"Ha! Ha!"* barked in discrete syllables, like an imitation of laughter.

"Harvey started frequenting the motel, usually to lounge by the pool with us in the afternoons. We—the residents, I mean—shared our fruits and vegetables with him, but his favorite thing is sunflowers. He is supposed to be a creature of the night, but that's changed too. He still takes daytime naps and stays up past midnight, but he isn't strictly nocturnal anymore.

"He enjoys the diner, and it used to be that when he wasn't here or in his park, he would be there, perched at the end of the counter, nibbling a salad. So—fast forward a bit—one day, he was sitting at the counter when a customer left a newspaper there. Just our local *Pie Town Gazette,* the only one we pay much attention to here. And one of our town fathers, M(1a), watched our little friend long enough to figure out he wasn't just staring at the paper but reading it. M(1a) was kind enough to help with the page-turning. After that, it just seemed natural to give him a job to do, so he could feel useful and have a role in town, like everyone else. He needed a name, so we could stop calling him just 'the hare.' Or, we thought so, and he seemed to agree."

Ava nodded. "It's good to have a name if you're going to live among people, and it's a good name too. Is Harvey happy here?"

"We think so. He has his own bungalow here at the motel now. We found him sleeping recently in a room we'd left open to air out, and we figured it was a hint. His place is the one with the sunflowers planted in the window box, right next to mine. I've filled his back courtyard with lettuces, carrots, and sunflowers too. Harvey knows to stay out of the cat vine grove, though. He made that mistake once when he wandered through the gate looking for a nibble." Evelyn shuddered at the memory and glanced out the window. She relaxed when she caught site of Harvey, who had returned from making his delivery and was sunning himself by the pool.

Evelyn turned her gaze to Ava, pinning her to her chair with a look no longer guileless but knowing.

"So, Ava, you saw our town, but your trucker friend did not."

Ava nearly dropped her coffee but caught herself just in time. "Can you read my thoughts?"

"Not all of them, no. Well, probably not." Evelyn laughed, but Ava didn't see the humor. "I have glimpses, it's true. It's how I knew you were on your way and that our birthday is coming up. You can do the same with me. I can teach you, or you will learn yourself. All in good time.

"Now, let me answer more of your questions by pointing out three simple facts. Firstly, you can see our town, an invisible oasis in the western desert. Secondly, you can see that our infinity pool is bottomless. Thirdly, you can see Harvey.

"Strangers do not see these things, Ava. Our regular visitors do not make the acquaintance of Harvey or experience the motel pool as anything unusual. You must know by now that you are neither a tourist nor a stranger here. Pie Town has extended a personal invitation to you. It is welcoming you with open arms."

"Evelyn, what is this place?" Ava whispered.

"This is your home, Ava darling. What else could it be?"

Ava stared at Evelyn, watching her refill their coffee cups and water glasses, but she didn't respond.

"I suppose it's more appropriate to say it's our birthplace, but isn't that the same thing?"

"No, that's not right," Ava replied, "I guess you don't know everything about me, after all." She felt relieved as though she'd reclaimed a piece of herself from Evelyn.

Evelyn tilted her head and squinted her eyes slightly, like a poker player about to lay down a royal flush and relishing the moment.

"All right, Ava. Here's how things unfolded outside of Pie Town: You—*we*—were born in the Catalina Island ER during an earthquake because Mama couldn't make it back to the mainland once her labor started. Who knew we'd be three weeks early? She had always said there was something odd about that island—"

"There was no *'we.'* It was just me. Mom had only one baby, then or ever." Ava's throat tightened, and her voice sounded higher than usual. She was sure that her mother would have told her about any other children, especially a twin. It was not only that Jeannie was bad at keeping secrets, but also that she would not have withheld something so important.

Evelyn smiled at Ava. "You're right. There was only one baby."

"I don't understand you, Evelyn." Ava could hear the frustration in her voice but made an effort to contain herself. "Please, just tell me what you mean instead of speaking in riddles. I already told you that I'm not good at word games, or mind games, or whatever you call this."

"I'm not toying with you, Ava. I'm trying to lead you backward slowly, one step at a time, so as not to startle you too much."

Ava stared at her. "Startle me how?"

The two women stared at each other for a long, silent moment, Ava's eyes wide with apprehension. Evelyn shook her head as if coming to a decision. "Like I said earlier," she replied, "I think it's better if I show you how things are here—"

"But you haven't shown me anything helpful," Ava argued, rubbing her palms against her jeans. She was beginning to feel antsy and knew it was more than the tingly current of the town. This conversation and Evelyn, in general, were overloading her. She needed to leave.

"Sure I have. You remembered something important about your time with Burke, the truck driver, didn't you?"

Ava thought back to their earlier conversation. She was certain she'd not shared anything about Burke with Evelyn.

"That's very specific, Evelyn. It would take more than a 'glimpse' into my thoughts for you to know that."

Evelyn cocked an eyebrow at Ava and shrugged.

"Never mind, Ava. What matters is that thanks to me, you remember what happened to you before your arrival here. Isn't that helpful?"

"I'm not sure what to think about you or this town, Evelyn. But one thing I do know is that you had nothing to do with my recalling my conversation with Burke."

"Are you sure about that?"

"I am, yes." Ava stood up from the table, tossing her napkin onto her plate. She began looking around for her backpack.

"It's on the couch, right over there," Evelyn said, answering a question Ava had not asked. Evelyn gestured vaguely toward the bar that created a divider between the lounge room and the kitchenette. A white leather couch sat in front of the bar, and Ava saw her backpack lying on its cushions.

"Stop doing that," Ava snapped, as she walked across the room to retrieve her pack.

"What?"

"You know *what*. Stop poking into my thoughts. They're private, and I hardly know you." Ava pulled her pack on and turned to Evelyn. "Besides, I don't believe half of what you say, especially about how I remembered Burke."

"Okay then, how did you remember?" Evelyn asked.

"I don't know. How does anyone remember anything? It just happens."

"Ava—" Evelyn began to stand, but Ava held up her palm like a crossing guard giving a warning.

"Sorry, but I need to go right now." Ava moved quickly to the door before Evelyn could stop her, opened it, and said, "Thanks for lunch," as she closed it behind her.

On her way to the camper, she stopped at Skylights Park and took Burke's phone out of her backpack, feeling desperate to talk to her mother. She flipped the phone open to see "No Service" displayed on the screen. Nevertheless, after pressing a few random buttons, the main menu came up, so that she could review the activity logs. She saw her home number listed at the top with no time stamp but with a duration of five minutes. *I had a five-minute conversation with Mom? What did we talk about?*

She stared at the screen for some time before it occurred to her to wonder, not what they'd discussed, but why she didn't remember making the call. She began pressing buttons again, trying to understand how the phone worked, until an ear-splitting squeal erupted from the speaker, causing her to toss the phone onto the grass. "No Service" flashed briefly onto the screen again before it went black, and Ava wondered if she'd killed it. Dead or alive, she was glad it had stopped squealing. She picked up the phone, flipped it closed, and stuffed it into her pack beneath her set of notebooks and her treasured, two-volume set of the National Audubon Society's *Field Guide to the Birds of North America*.

Eight

Once back at the camper, Ava took a shower and changed into clean jeans. She started to roll down the loose waist, as she'd been doing for the past couple of months, but found it no longer necessary. Her jeans fit perfectly. She wondered how that could be, after just one night and half a day of regular meals and crazy amounts of pie. She'd avoided making eye contact with full-length mirrors recently, knowing that besides looking gaunt she was also becoming haggard, her usually fair skin red and rough from overexposure, and her hair dry and lifeless. She looked around the Airstream for a mirror and found one in the back of a closet. Propping it against the wall, she stared at her reflection.

I look healthy again. I look perfectly like me. By some magic or miracle—Ava wasn't sure she knew the difference—she looked as fresh and vibrant as she had when she left L.A. She enjoyed a brief celebration dance with her reflection before recalling that she also looked perfectly like Evelyn. Ava looked through her clothes and selected a white, fitted t-shirt illustrated with an American robin perched on her nest, guarding her eggs. Surely, Evelyn did not collect bird wear? Ava considered this as she made herself a cup of tea and settled down to write.

Home . . . Home . . . Home. The word coursed through her head as she struggled to get her thoughts onto paper. She grappled for an analogy to describe how it felt. *A ping pong ball, a pinball, a missile?* No, it was like Marvin the Martian zipping around in his cartoon spaceship. Ava imagined "Home or Bust" emblazoned on a banner trailing behind him.

She had always liked Marvin best of all the Looney Tunes characters, especially when he said things like, "I think man is the most interesting insect on earth." She drew a tiny Marvin in her notebook, and then set her pen down and stared at the otherwise empty page.

After Evelyn had said "this is your home," Ava had begun to feel increasingly desperate to be alone, to think things through and make lists—however many lists it took to unravel the knots in her brain. Her usually well-ordered mind was in chaos, until she remembered, "M(1a) was kind enough to help with the page-turning." Ava pulled her purple and white coupon out of her notebook and verified that it had been signature-stamped by M(1a), whom Evelyn had called one of the town fathers. She'd referred to the two women in the photos as the "founding mothers," making it sound as though the population consisted of one big family.

She picked up her pen again and selected a sheet of sherbet-orange stationery. She knew that when she finished writing she would feel better for having composed order from disarray. She sifted through her thoughts, deciding which of many questions most immediately concerned her, and came up with six:

> *Who is Evelyn to me?*
> *How could I forget talking to Mom?*
> *Why am I drawn to that pool?*
> > *(Did I truly almost drown?)*
> > *(Why can't I remember what happened down there?)*
> *Why does this strange place feel more like home than home?*

She wrote her queries several times in delicate script, until they covered the paper, and then thought about where to begin finding answers. Investigation was not her forte. She'd been keen to travel and observe the lives of others but only from the safety of her silent inner perch. She wasn't one to pry information out of people. However, the diner was the sort of place where one might eavesdrop discreetly. Maybe she could learn something over dinner.

Ava folded her list into a paper crane—an enduring symbol of happiness, peace, and good fortune—and held it on her palm. She'd used her sherbet-orange stationery and written her notes in sea-blue ink. The sense of order she'd achieved with her list had been transformed into mystery once again, but it was a peaceful mystery. The crane sat in her hand as independent of her as if they'd only just met, its integrity complete, its self-possession undeniable. The letters revealed on the bird's wings, tail, legs, body, and head were like secret messages whose codes Ava could not break. She turned the crane over in her palm, whispering the words like a breathy incantation: "Evelyn, Mom, drown, remember, home . . ."

The paper wings fluttered. The crane was aloft, hovering just above Ava's right palm so lightly that it barely displaced the air. It opened its eyes and then its beak, neither of which Ava had made, and looked at her with intent for several slow heartbeats. When it found its voice, the paper throat produced a raspy susurration, not like a real crane at all. It delivered its words with a halting urgency, and so quietly that Ava strained to hear: "Remember home . . . Remember home . . . Remember . . ." It petered out, and Ava half expected it to fall over dead from its effort, but the crane had not finished. Its final words were a lamentation: "Ava," the bird gasped, "this . . . is . . . not . . . your . . . story."

Nine

Ava opened her eyes. She was on the couch but slumped over. She knew she'd been asleep for quite a while because night had fallen. Immediately, she began to look around for the sherbet-orange crane, but it was nowhere. No crane, no list.

"No way," she said to herself, but not only to herself.

She felt, rather than heard, Harvey at the screen door. He stood staring at her somberly. Ava was not sure how long he'd been there. She wondered fleetingly what Harvey knew and understood about Pie Town and Evelyn, but she dismissed these questions from her mind when she realized how innocent he looked.

And what of the crane? She decided it would turn up later, probably. Her life was full of these types of incidences, such as when she would drop a pen on the floor, and not find it until months later, when it reappeared in her underwear drawer. Probably, it was that kind of thing. She knew the origami crane couldn't have flown away; surely, she'd dreamed that.

I was awake, though, when it spoke to me.

Ava scrubbed her face with her hands and shook off the last vestiges of sleep as best she could before turning to greet her visitor.

"Hi, Harvey. Do you have a message for me?"

Harvey looked at the ground. She tried again.

"Would you like to come in?"

Ava opened the screen, and Harvey leaped over the threshold. He glanced around before taking a seat on the couch cushion next to Ava. Ava wasn't sure about the etiquette of entertaining a jackrabbit, so she offered the one thing that came to mind.

"Would you like a carrot?"

Harvey sat up straight and tall then, ears erect, eyes wide, and nose twitching.

"I'll take that as a *yes*," Ava said. She rustled through the refrigerator and pulled out carrots and lettuce, which she cut up and arranged on a plate for him.

"Sorry, I don't have any sunflowers, but hopefully this will do."

While Harvey munched his food, Ava stared at him, wondering who'd dressed him for his visit. He wore a large silk scarf, tied in an elegant bow around his neck. She reached for one end of the fabric, turning it over in her fingers.

"Harvey, that's just beautiful, and it's one of my favorite colors too." Ava gestured to the robin's eggs on her shirt. Harvey's scarf was the same blue as the eggs and speckled like a real shell. Near his throat, the silk was loosely knotted and pinned with a cameo of creamy glazed porcelain. She peered closer, expecting to see a hare silhouette painted there, but it was a nest filled with broken shells.

"Looks like we have the same taste in clothes," Ava said, smiling at him. "Where'd your mama bird and her chicks fly off to?"

Harvey held his silence but extended his right front paw to her. Ava took the paw and surprised herself by leaning over to kiss it. She looked at the gentle hare, whose gaze was unblinking.

"Okay," Ava said, replying to a question that had not been asked, "Where are we going?"

Without hesitation, Harvey leaped from the couch and bounded down the stairs of the Airstream. Ava skipped after him, slamming the door of the camper behind her. He slowed for Ava to catch up and tried to shorten his leaps so she wouldn't fall behind. Still, they were moving fast enough that Ava was practically running.

"Harvey, I only have two legs!"

As they turned out of the RV park and reached the sidewalk, Ava stopped. The Flying Saucer Diner was lit up across the street, illuminating three bowler-capped backs through the plate glass windows. Ava wondered if it was the same group from this morning and then figured it had to be. How many bowler-capped triplets could there be in one small town? Then again, how many sets of twins had she come across so far? Besides Evelyn and herself, there were Jasmine and Julie, and then these guys, who were twins-plus-one. She wondered if they always wore those hats. It certainly made them easy to recognize.

She could see Julie at the diner's counter. There were at least two dozen customers inside, no doubt enjoying conversation with friends over pancakes or pie and coffee. Even from this distance, Ava could feel the cheerful hum of the place. She glanced up and down the sidewalk and saw that there were people everywhere now, out walking in pairs and trios, and slipping in and out of the local establishments; but none of them came near where she stood with Harvey.

Ava was reminded of a cuckoo clock she'd seen once, as a child, in the Christmas window display at a department store. The clock had seemed huge, towering over her as she peered through the glass. When the chimes struck the magic hour, secret doors sprang open, and all the hidden folk of the village came out strolling, ice skating, riding toy trains, and singing carols. Ava had felt enchanted, and it had taken her mother's best bribes to coax her away from the window after an hour of watching the mechanical wonder.

There was something similar here, she thought, in watching the Pie Towners pour into the local thoroughfare, to go about their business or pleasure. Superficially, the scene was just as convivial as the private world of the cuckoo clock but, instead of delighting her, it unsettled her. Looking around, she could see the silhouettes of several dozen people moving under the streetlights but could make out none of their faces. Ava wondered why she had encountered so few people since her arrival and, for a paranoid moment, considered that maybe they were avoiding her.

Then she remembered that she was not important enough to avoid, and that made her feel a bit better. Still, it was peculiar. After breakfast at the diner this morning, she'd walked up and down this street without seeing a single soul, until Harvey had approached her in the park with his message from Evelyn. Where had everyone been then? It was true that she wasn't the most sociable person in the world, but she was used to brief exchanges when mixing with locals in a new town. Here, the only people who'd spoken to her since her arrival had been Jasmine, Jack, Julie, and Evelyn. Harvey communicated eloquently with no words at all.

Harvey tried to chivvy her along. Ava could sense his impatience, but she turned back again to stare at the diner's flying-saucer-shaped neon sign advertising "Fresh Hot Pie!" Shouldn't she stop in for pie and coffee, and park herself near some locals? Hadn't that been her original plan, to listen? She'd let that idea fly out the window when Harvey arrived at the door.

As if sensing that he was losing her attention, Harvey jumped behind Ava and stretched up on his hind legs to tap her lower back with his paws, prodding her forward.

"Sorry, Harvey. I got distracted."

As she trotted along behind him, Ava wondered where they were going. Harvey was leading her toward the opposite end of town from where she was staying—past the drug store, the record shop, and a restaurant called Cafe Z that had a tropical beach scene painted across its plate-glass facade. Had that cafe been there before? Ava wasn't sure, but she remembered then that she knew something about the owner. What was it that she knew? The information seemed just out of reach, but then she had it. *It's Jack's place,* she recalled. When she'd asked Julie where she could find Jack, Julie had said that he and his wife owned Cafe Z.

But there was more that she knew too. Ava slowed her pace and backtracked a few feet to stand in front of the cafe. Its raffia shades were down, and no light emanated from within. Ava stared at the festive mural as she rifled through the contents of her mind. Evelyn had said, "Jack is the only one in town who wears a watch," but Ava struggled to remember when she had said this.

"Harvey, wait!" Ava called out, glancing around for him, but then she saw that he hadn't gone far. He was standing still, a hare-shaped shadow under the marquee of the cinema, two doors down from the cafe. The record shop sat between them, closed for the night. Harvey took a little leap toward the streetlight so that she could see him clearly and then cocked his right ear as if asking her why.

She repeated, "Please wait."

Harvey hopped to her side and stood up on his back feet. He held out a paw, which Ava accepted, and they stood staring at the cafe together. Although seeing it had triggered the memory of an earlier conversation with Evelyn, the actual contents of that discussion had entirely slipped her mind. *How could I have forgotten that too?* She wondered if the last few months of desperado living had caught up with her and damaged her brain, the part where memories lived.

Within moments, the dam burst and the conversation flooded her mind with full lights, color, and sound. They had been in Evelyn's room at the motel, and Evelyn had just licked chocolate meringue pie off her fingers. She'd landed Ava with one of her hard, unblinking stares.

Evelyn had said, "this ain't California," and the next thing Ava knew she was lost in reverie, lulled by Evelyn's Southern lilt and penetrating gaze.

No, that wasn't true. Ava had not been daydreaming at all. She and Evelyn had been talking the whole time.

Ten

"Ava darlin', this ain't California."

"No, of course, it isn't," Ava replied. "I've only been here one night and half a day, but I guess I know that. L.A. is strange, but this place is way stranger. Things just seem to pop up out of nowhere around here. Do other visitors comment on this?"

"Sure they do. It used to be much more like that before the founding mothers paid the town a visit," Evelyn replied.

"When was that?" Ava asked.

"You mean outer-desert time? In your terms, that would be something like last year, or last month, or a week ago maybe . . ." Evelyn trailed off as if speaking a foreign language that she only half remembered.

Ava must have looked dumbfounded, because Evelyn shrugged and tossed up her hands, before attempting to clarify: "Ava, here in Pie Town, it is always *now*. We talk about events that have or have not occurred but as far as when, specifically, they have or have not occurred, that's tricky. The town resists such efforts to pin it down. We who live here tend to describe things simply as happening 'before' or 'after,' but we struggle when asked to itemize minutes, hours, days, weeks, and years.

"Time here flows like a meandering river. Sometimes, it seems not to flow at all. Our coarse observations tell us that the weather never changes, the grass never grows, the buildings never need a coat of paint, and we never grow old. And yet, sometimes we feel that these things are happening, but so incrementally that we cannot perceive them with our limited senses. We don't know for certain. We adjust our rhythms by sunrises and sunsets, but who can say it's not the same sunrise, the same sunset, every time? Do you understand?"

"No," Ava answered. She could not have said more even if she had known what to say. Her throat had gone dry, and her skin prickled. She still felt tingly inside, but that was starting to seem normal.

"It's difficult to grasp the paradoxical nature of Pie Town, especially when one is from the outer desert. It's better to experience it yourself by staying here a while. You remember the photo I showed you in the lobby of our founding mothers, Lenie and Rachel, taken when they were about our age?"

Ava nodded.

"Well, here's perhaps the best example of the unfathomable nature of time in Pie Town. Lenie and Rachel were born here, in the very town that they would not bring to life until they were young adults at college. Wrap your head around that if you can."

Ava stared at Evelyn for a while before answering, "I can't wrap my head around any of this, Evelyn. I am not a physicist. My scientific interests are ornithology and botany. I read Rachel Carson and Florence Merriam Bailey. I sketch birds and plants and write lists and fold origami. This stuff is way beyond my understanding. I would say that I feel like I've slipped into a dream and can't wake up, except that's not true. I'm wide awake but way off-kilter." Ava rubbed her eyes and face with her hands—a gesture that was becoming more frequent the longer she stayed in Pie Town.

Evelyn backtracked, looking apologetic. "I'm sorry. You asked about the town's spatial stability, so I thought I would try to explain its temporal existence, too, but I can see I am overloading you. We local folk are limited in our knowledge too. Most of what we think we know is speculative, based on M(1a)'s theories. He writes them up and publishes them in the *Gazette*. It makes for interesting reading, but there's no way to know whether it's an accurate representation of our world. We have nothing to compare it to, except for what we've gathered from our collection of cultural artifacts, such as our movies over at the cinema, and what we learn from our visitors.

"Let's go back to our founding mothers. As I was saying, their initial visit seemed to have a stabilizing effect on the dreamscape."

"Dreamscape?" Ava asked.

"Yes, that's how Pie Town started, from what we know: psychic phenomena manifested on the physical plane. Alas, this particular spot was already in use."

Ava nodded as if this made sense, so Evelyn kept going. "M(1a) reckons that the spatial disturbances of the landscape—things popping in and out—were due not only to the original drawings having been completed in stages but also to overloading the points of connection between the dreamscape and the intergalactic superhighway. Both are highly trafficked, as you can imagine.

"Once Lenie and Rachel brought the town to life—right on top of the superhighway's earth replenishment point—it opened the plane for other people's dreams to begin landing here, too, which resulted in utter chaos. Everybody was confused for I don't know how long. Then, overnight, order was restored: the town tossed out the interlopers and set up protective boundaries. But that came after Lenie and Rachel left on their first indefinite holiday."

"Which was, like, either an hour before I arrived or ten years ago?" Ava chimed in, resenting her own sarcasm but needing to vent a little.

Evelyn beamed at her and said, "Exactly!" as though Ava were an unusually gifted student making a clever point.

"M(1a) says that the superhighway and the dreamscape were made possible by the emergent properties of this particular spot in the galaxy, but that did not mean they harmonized easily; rather, they seemed to fight for dominance like two cats vying for territory. One day, this was just a rest-and-refill station servicing space travelers, who were mostly from Galactica Five and Orlon Six. The next day, it was a full-fledged town overflowing with sleepwalking strangers wandering in from the desert or manifesting out of thin air. Can you imagine? Everything was in a state of flux.

"I am happy to say that, now, most of our town is here most of the time, instead of fading in and out on a whim. That could be a bit disconcerting even for those of us who live here, to tell you the truth. But it's still the case that different types of folks experience Pie Town differently. It is not the same town for all beings, and we don't all interact with it in the same way."

Evelyn looked at Ava as though waiting for a response, but Ava was silent.

"Anyhoo, perhaps it isn't obvious, but we are a proud and efficient community. We have no clocks, but Pie Town runs like clockwork." Evelyn paused to laugh at her joke before continuing. Ava stared at her. "Jack is the only one in town who wears a watch. Of course, the hands don't move anymore, but he is sentimental about it because it belonged to his father."

Ava continued to stare but remained speechless. Evelyn cleared her throat.

"We remain a superhighway stopover, and we've become a popular tourist destination for interplanetary pie lovers. We host a tidy and well-managed dreamscape that is now—thank our lucky stars—by invitation only. I should say the town hosts the dreamscape. The rest of us are like the permanent cast and crew in a movie that never ends."

Ava bobbed her head once, to show she was listening. Yes, she could see Evelyn as an actress, and herself unwittingly lost in a movie.

"Once the founding mothers graced us with their presence—" Evelyn paused to place her hand over her heart and bow her head briefly before continuing "—the town settled down and became much more reliable. Pie Town no longer depends solely on the psyches of its founders but thrives on the energy of all who live and visit here. It's a symbiotic relationship, I guess you'd say. Perhaps that explains why those of us who live here are particular about our guests."

"Are you saying that the town communicates with its citizens?" Ava asked, glad to have found her voice again.

"Not in words but, yes, it communicates. And, while the town is less reliant on our founders nowadays, I contend that the fruit has not fallen far from the maternal tree. Pie Town is generous, kind-hearted, enthusiastic, and reclusive. It listens to too much Bob Marley, which drives us all a bit mad, but at least that's confined to the cafe. In fact, all our music is restricted to the cafe, the diner, and the record shop. We are working to change that. In the meantime, if you put on a record at the cafe, don't be surprised to hear Bob Marley and the Wailers coming out of the speakers."

"Evelyn, you said that visitors nowadays arrive here by invitation only, right?"

Evelyn nodded.

Ava wondered why she felt compelled to keep up with her end of this loony conversation. She didn't believe half of what Evelyn was saying, and that was the half she understood. She was pretty sure that the half she didn't understand was likewise unbelievable. She didn't want to say that, though. She needed time alone to think things over and make notes. Instead, she said, "What about me? I didn't receive an invitation."

"That's because you didn't need one," Evelyn replied.

"Oh."

She must have looked stupefied, or like she thought Evelyn had lost her mind because Evelyn acted quickly to change the conversation.

"Shoot, Ava, just look at you. What is the matter with me? It's all too much, isn't it?" Evelyn's voice twanged with concern as she began waving her arms across Ava's face in a way that made Ava think she was chasing a fly or mosquito. She finished up this performance with the words, "Let's just forget this for now."

Eleven

Ava looked at Harvey, who stood patiently next to her, still holding her hand but staring up at the clear night sky. She reached down to stroke his head before looking up herself, to see what he was seeing.

"Oh, my stars, Harvey," Ava said, startling herself with how easily she mimicked her lookalike's accent. Harvey's ears twitched in response as he thumped his back left foot, making Ava laugh.

"That is what Evelyn would say, isn't it? Something like: 'Oh, my stars, just look at all those pretty little spaceships!'" The glossy candy-colored saucers zoomed past thrillingly, and Ava wondered if this was what she'd missed last night by turning in early. "It's only the superhighway, Harv, nothing to worry about, right? It's like L.A. with less traffic."

Harvey tilted his head to peer up at Ava and tugged gently on her arm until they were moving again. As they approached the cinema's ticket booth, Ava assumed Harvey was taking her to the movies. She waited behind Harvey at the booth, its dark interior preventing her from seeing whoever might be there. Neither did she see any money exchanged. Nevertheless, when Harvey turned back to face her, he was holding a single ticket in his teeth. Ava took the ticket and watched him hop away. She didn't call after him but stood examining her ticket. Later, she would find herself missing his company but grateful that he hadn't been there for the experience.

Ava couldn't remember the first time she'd gone to the cinema. As far as she knew, it was something she and

Jeannie had always done. She noticed that Pie Town's Cinema Retrograde was markedly like The Ritz Revival House back home that she'd gone to her entire life. The original Art Deco style of both buildings was perfectly maintained.

She wondered what she was going to see, and why she was the only person in the audience. There hadn't been a movie title on the marquee, just random letters and numbers that looked like nonsense to Ava. Her ticket was the kind that came on a big roll, printed in consecutive numbers and the words "Admit One," like those handed out at carnivals and fairgrounds. Evelyn had mentioned that she'd seen the movie *Harvey* here. That was promising.

The lights went down, and a cartoon advertising concession-stand snacks filled the screen. The dancing and singing popcorn, candy, and soda made Ava wish she'd parted with some of her cash and gotten one of each. She and Jeannie had often smuggled in homemade treats, only splurging at the movies when times were especially good. She was glad that the heady scent of fresh buttery popcorn wasn't wafting into the cinema. That might have done her in.

The cartoon ended, and the cinema was dark and quiet for several seconds. Then she saw light flickering through blank film, and the feature started, without a title or list of credits. It opened on a grainy black-and-white print, with the camera focused too closely on the back of a woman walking away. A burst of feminine laughter filled the speakers. The woman pulled ahead and then turned toward the camera, still laughing, and Ava could see that it was Jeannie: young, fragile, heavily-pregnant Jeannie, as she was before Ava appeared in her life.

Ava sucked in her breath and sat up straight, her hands gripping the arms of her chair. Her mother was saying something, but the sound of it didn't reach the camera. When Jeannie turned away again, the camera pulled back far enough for Ava to recognize the setting. Her mother was walking up the ramp to board the Catalina Island ferry.

The film jumped to Jeannie on the boat, leaning against the railing. She was relaxed, with her eyes closed and her face turned to the sun, but the water was choppy, and the wind lifted her hair. She'd had a pixie cut then, like Mia Farrow. Ava had seen the photos and thought it suited her fine bones and delicate features, but Jeannie hadn't liked it and had never cut it that short again.

The film hiccupped again. Jeannie was walking some distance ahead of the camera. Ava could see that she was wearing hiking books along with a short peasant dress that stretched taut against her belly. She smiled at her mother's version of practical dressing. Again, the surroundings were familiar. Jeannie was making her way up the staircase of the Wrigley Memorial. Every few steps, she'd turn around and say something to the camera, but none of her words were discernible. The sounds the camera had picked were the gusting wind, rustling trees, and birdsong, along with the scraping of leather soles against rough stone. Ava wondered who had been on the other side of that camera, to whose footsteps she was listening.

Once again, the film made a jump that indicated splicing, but this time it cut to a different setting. Two young women were sitting at a table in a cafe. They leaned in together with their heads down, looking at a spiral notebook laid out on the table. Ava sat back and relaxed a little, relieved to see that she didn't know them; or, she didn't *think* she knew them. It was hard to say with their hair hanging in their faces. It didn't take long to notice that, unlike Jeannie, the two girls (about her own age, she thought) did not act as if they were aware of being filmed. They did not look up at the camera and smile, as her mother had. They were laughing, although, as with Jeannie, their voices were not discernible. One ran her finger over stick figures on a hand-drawn map, while the other sketched in additional objects that Ava couldn't make out. The one with the pencil paused and then said something, tapping the page emphatically with the lead point. The camera shook in response to the tapping.

Another hiccup and the camera was back on Jeannie. This time, she was sitting at the top of the memorial's steps, and everything around her was shaking. Ava heard rumbling and knew it was the earthquake hitting the island. One of Jeannie's hands was on the step next to her, and the other was on her belly. Her eyes were wide with fear.

Ava brought her hands to her mouth, her own eyes mimicking her mother's. She could hear her heartbeat pounding in her ears and thought she might throw up. She reminded herself that she knew—of *course*, she knew!—how this story ended. Jeannie would be fine. Wouldn't she? In real life, she had been, but was this movie following real life?

The film jumped back to the girls in the cafe. They were both talking animatedly now, the one with the pencil still adding to the drawing.

Ava was making herself take deep breaths, but her whole body seemed to be leaning toward the film, and she held tightly to the armrests of her chair.

When Jeannie reappeared, she was in the ER on a gurney, still talking soundlessly to the camera, while everything shook and rumbled around her. Ava could hear the rumbling but nothing else. Jeannie stopped talking, overcome by a contraction.

Ava sat back in her chair, pulled her legs up in front of her, and wrapped her arms around them until she had made herself as small as possible.

The movie began to progress quickly, one brief scene after another. Nurses were attending Jeannie, and then a doctor. More contractions. Finally, a baby in her arms.

Ava gasped. Her heart fluttered. *Me,* she thought, *that's me she's holding.* She relaxed, finally, and smiled without realizing it.

The camera zoomed in on the completed birth certificate that a nurse was passing to her mother to review.

CATALINA ISLAND MEDICAL CENTER
LOS ANGELES COUNTY, CALIFORNIA

CERTIFICATE OF BIRTH

This Certifies that <u>LOUISE LOUISE PEMBROKE</u> was born to mother, <u>JEAN LOUISE PEMBROKE</u>, and father, <u>UNKNOWN</u>, in this hospital at <u>11:00 A.M.</u> on <u>SUNDAY</u>, the <u>11TH</u> day of <u>FEBRUARY 1996</u>.

In Witness Whereof, the said Hospital has caused this Certificate to be signed by its duly authorized officer and its Official Seal to be hereunto affixed.

Blanche Adair, RN, MSN
Nurse Superintendent

Dr. Lisette Bonaventura, M.D.
Attending Physician

Ava squinted at the film, trying to make sense of the certificate. *Why does it say "Louise Louise" where it should say "Ava Louise"?* Before she could study it further, the image was gone, leaving Ava with a lingering impression of it looking like her Pie Town coupon: it was plain, lacking any flourishes whatsoever, and she could have sworn it was printed in purple ink. She'd not seen the hospital seal on it, either.

The film hiccupped its way back to the girls in the cafe and lingered there. The two of them, one a willowy blonde and the other a petite brunette, were sitting back, sipping coffee and chatting, while holding their notebook between them. Ava recognized them now that she could see their faces fully. They were the girls in the photos in the motel. It made no sense. What did they have to do with her mom? The dark-haired girl scribbled with her pencil on a page of the open notebook, and the camera shook. The room didn't shake, just the camera, which made Ava wonder if the camera had been embedded in the notebook. Was that possible?

The setting changed again, and Ava felt as if she'd been plunged into a sci-fi movie. She was overcome by vertigo as her perspective shifted from third-person observer to that of the camera itself, which was now soaring through outer space, transmitting images of distant stars and planets. Earth zoomed into view, before drawing closer at a terrifying speed. Ava scrambled onto her knees in the cushioned chair of the cinema, holding tightly to the back of the seat in front of her. She gasped when the camera shot through the planet's atmosphere, expecting virtual annihilation, which didn't come.

The camera maintained its course, slower now, falling vertically toward land. It was engulfed by night, but there must have been a full moon because the sprawling desert was easy to see as it came into view: mountains, cactuses, scrub—and the town chapel. There it was, clear as anything, the old chapel standing alone in the stark desert, illuminated by stars and moonlight—

Ava shot to her feet as the camera slammed into the ground, shuddering as it burrowed deeper and deeper into the soil. After the vast silence of space and the eerie nothingness of passing through the atmosphere, the noise of the crash was deafening. But this lasted only seconds before the screen went black. Ava heard a coyote howl in the distance, and then there was silence.

Ava blinked, disoriented at the lights coming on. The projector clicked to a stop. She got to her feet and walked out into the lobby, feeling wobbly. No one had taken her ticket when she'd entered the cinema, but the girl who must have sold it to Harvey was standing behind the counter, with her arms crossed, and not looking particularly friendly.

Ava was relieved to see that this clerk looked nothing like Jasmine and Julie, or Evelyn and herself. She was tall and thin as a blade of grass, with a pert face framed by choppy, electric-blue hair. Ava thought it possible that the girl's expression could be read as *go away,* but she decided to ignore this and approached the counter. She leaned in just close enough to read the clerk's name tag. Beneath the words "Cinema Retrograde," which were engraved in black script and surrounded by gold stars, Ava saw the name "Angie" spelled out in block letters.

"Angie . . ." Ava began. She wanted to say something, but words failed her, as they so often did when face-to-face with other people. She stood at the counter, staring down at the boxes of Jelly Babies and Junior Mints, biding her time.

Angie said, "Yeah, that's me. So, what do you think?"

Ava was startled. She glanced up at the girl. What did she think? Good question.

"You want some candy to take home, or not? I've got to close up for the night, so if you could make up your mind, that would be great," Angie said. She didn't sound angry, Ava thought, just impatient.

Ava cleared her throat and tried to keep her voice steady. "You know, that movie wasn't quite right. I mean the bit about my mother and me, for example. I don't know how you got that footage of Mom, but my first name isn't Louise."

For a moment, Ava thought the woman wouldn't respond. She seemed to stare right through her. Ava watched as Angie reached into the glass cabinet and plucked out a box of Cracker Jack and a packet of Junior Mints. She pushed them across the counter to Ava and said, "Have these, from the house. Goodnight now."

Angie started to walk off.

"Wait, please!" Ava shouted. Angie turned halfway, waiting for Ava to continue. "I don't understand. What was my mother doing in that movie? How do you people know my mom?" she implored.

Angie gave Ava a sideways glance before turning away, tossing her reply over her shoulder. "Ava, this is not your story."

"What is that supposed to mean?" Ava screamed the question, startling herself, but Angie had disappeared behind a curtain at the back of the refreshments station with an air of finality.

The building was still. Ava had been the only customer, and the only staff member she'd seen was Angie. Ava heard the *clack, clack, clack* of industrial lights being shut off, row by row, and soon stood alone in the silent dark. "Nice," she muttered. She grabbed the candy off the counter and left the cinema even more confused than when she'd entered. Only later, rethinking the exchange, did she remember that Angie had called her by name.

Twelve

Ava was relieved to find Harvey waiting for her on the sidewalk. Harvey reached out a paw, and Ava grasped it lightly before giving it a squeeze. She did not know why her friend had brought her to the movies and given her a ticket, nor did she know why he had not accompanied her inside. But looking at him now as he peered up at her in his gentle manner, she could not believe that he had known what she would see and experience inside, or that it might disturb her.

Ava bent down to Harvey's level so that she could look him in the eye. "Did Evelyn send you to me? Did she tell you to take me to the movies and pick me up afterward?" Ava asked. She spoke softly. She did not want Harvey to feel that she was accusing him of acting in bad faith, or that she was rejecting his friendship. Ava had enjoyed so few genuine friendships in her life that she was grateful when someone made an effort, and if that someone happened to be a thoughtful hare, that was even better.

Harvey moved close to Ava and answered her questions by nuzzling her nose with his own, and then placing his forehead on her forehead. Ava hugged Harvey, overwhelmed by his gesture. As she stood up, she heard someone calling to her from a few feet away.

"Ava?" Jack called.

Ava stood up straight and turned around to find Jack holding open the door to Cafe Z.

"Hello, Mr. Jack," she said, and then felt silly for it. "I mean Jack. May I call you Jack? I don't know your last name."

"My family name is Sparks, but everyone calls me Jack. You can call me anything you like, just don't call me late for dinner," Jack replied, smiling at Ava.

Ava stared at him. "Why would I do that?" she asked.

"It's an old joke. Never mind. How about you come on inside? I've got an empty house and a full pot of hot chocolate. Can I tempt you?" Jack asked.

"That sounds good. Thanks." Ava turned to take Harvey's paw and lead him inside, but he was gone. "Harvey?" she called.

"Who are you looking for?" Jack asked.

"Harvey, of course. Don't you know Harvey? The messenger hare?"

"Harvey, the messenger hare? No, I'm afraid I haven't had the pleasure," Jack answered.

"He was just here. You didn't see me hugging him? A black-tailed jackrabbit, about three feet tall, wearing a billowy blue scarf?" She was staring hard at Jack, who cleared his throat and glanced up and down the street before answering.

"Righty-o, Ava, I believe you. But I don't know Harvey, and I haven't seen him. You may have gleaned by now that there's a lot about this town that you don't understand yet. Frankly, there's a lot about it that none of us understand. If you come inside, I could help you out with a few things, at least."

Ava hesitated, looking up and down the street again, just in case. One by one, the street lights switched off, until there was only the moon to see by. All the businesses that Ava could see were closed and their windows curtained. If Harvey remained nearby, he'd been swallowed by the night. Ava felt bereft and, for once, did not want to be alone. She walked over to where Jack stood holding the door open for her.

"Why'd the street lights go out?" she asked him.

"It's that time of night," Jack explained. "They run on a cycle, switching on at twilight and off around midnight or thereabouts."

"How do you know when it's midnight? How does anyone here know that?" Ava asked, stepping over the threshold of Cafe Z.

"We know because the street lights go out," Jack answered, laughing lightly. Then, more seriously, he added, "We order our days by the sun and our nights by the moon and stars, as all other creatures have done since the beginning of life on this planet."

Ava stared at him, struck by the poetic simplicity of his answer. It was what Evelyn had told her, too, that people here organized their lives by sunrises and sunsets. She nodded at Jack and stepped into the cafe.

"Anyway, I'm glad you're here, Ava." Jack pulled the door closed, locking it. Ava paused, staring at the locked door, and did not move farther inside.

"I'm closed now," Jack explained, "but I saw you outside and wanted to have a chat. You are perfectly safe with me."

"Okay," Ava answered, still not moving. She glanced around the cafe, most of which was lit by candles, creating a romantic ambiance. The melting-wax scents of coconut, vanilla, and orange blossoms wafted over to where they stood.

"How about we have a seat at one of the tables?" Jack suggested, gesturing to a round, rattan table in a corner near the kitchen. "Just so you know, I am crazily happily married and not looking to change that."

That could have been a line, but Ava didn't think so. He actually looked crazily happily married when he said it. She relaxed and smiled at him. "And I'm crazily happily gay, just so you know," she replied.

Jack laughed. "We'll both be safe then. Sit right down over here while I fetch the hot chocolate. You want brandy with yours? Or in it? Sounds wrong to me, but my wife Annie loves it that way."

"No thanks. I don't usually drink alcohol. It can make me loopy, like someone cross-wired my circuits. Then I drop off to sleep for eighteen hours or more." Ava sighed and sank into the cushion of a rattan armchair.

She watched Jack walk behind a diner-style counter and enter the kitchen, before taking in the rest of her surroundings. The cafe looked nothing like any of the other places she'd seen in Pie Town. It was decked out in a tropical theme, including fake Raffia palms with stuffed monkeys clinging to the trunks, rattan tables and chairs, African tribal rugs, and a bold mural painted on the surrounding walls.

Next to Ava's chair was a burnt-orange Planet lamp, which she recognized because Jeannie had bought two of them at a resale shop and refurbished them for home. Ava switched on the lamp and focused it on the part of the mural nearest her. The bottom of the wall up to about four feet was all ocean. Ava could see dolphins, turtles, and fish swimming its length before continuing the journey on the next wall. The mural had been painted from the perspective of the ocean, so she could imagine herself out on the water, in a gently rocking boat, miles from shore. Everywhere she looked was sea and sky, with a thin strip of golden beach dividing them. Clusters of tiny grass huts decorated the sand, while bright tropical birds soared overhead.

"It's Zanzibar," Jack said, returning to their table carrying a tray. "'Cafe Z' stands for Zanzibar. I always meant to go there, to the real place, you know. But things didn't work out that way."

Ava wasn't sure what to say, but she knew one thing for certain about that part of the world. "They have great birds there."

Jack nodded. "Yes, and beautiful fish too." He began filling a round, earthenware mug for her, "This drink is a house specialty. We call it Zanzibar Spiced Chocolate."

"What's in it?" Ava asked. She lifted her mug and sniffed. "It sure smells good."

"The spices of Zanzibar," Jack replied. "We've got cinnamon, nutmeg, cloves, and just a dash of black pepper in there. Annie makes our fluffy marshmallows. What do you think?" He sat down across from her, moving other items he'd brought from the kitchen off the tray and onto the table. Ava eyed a plate of sandwiches and cakes and realized how hungry she was.

Passing her a plate, Jack said, "Please dig in. It'll just go to waste otherwise."

"I think this is the best hot chocolate I've ever had in my whole life."

Jack beamed at her. "That's what I like to hear."

"You made all this for me?" Ava was incredulous.

"No. I'd be lying if I said that. I was going to go around and look for you tomorrow, but I didn't expect to see you here tonight."

"Who were you expecting?"

"No one. Annie and I made too much food. We were set to cater an afternoon lunch party for folks over at the visitor center. We got a last-minute message saying that only half the crew had shown up, so we left this tray of goodies here."

Ava sat upright in her chair, which creaked in response. "I heard from Julie at the diner that there's a visitor center. Why haven't I seen it? I've walked the town, and it only takes half an hour to see the whole thing."

"No, not really."

"Not really what?"

"It doesn't take only half an hour to see the whole thing. You just . . . You can't see the whole thing, is the thing. Not yet, anyway."

"Oh," Ava said, wondering if more buildings would have popped up by the time she got up in the morning.

Jack poured rum into a snifter and lit up a joint. That was when Ava noticed that she was the only one eating. She set down her vegetable sandwich and looked at him.

"Do you smoke?" he asked, widening his eyes at her while passing the joint across the table.

"No, never. I think I'm probably weird enough without the dope." Ava slapped her hand over her mouth to stop more words from slipping out.

Jack laughed. It was a big, good-natured guffaw that made Ava laugh too.

"Sorry," she said. "I didn't mean that you're weird or anything."

"I am just about as weird as they come, Ava, if by 'weird' you mean not fitting into the regular habits and expectations of most people my age. All of Pie Town's inhabitants are weird in some way, but we like to think we're harmless and lovable," Jack said. "That's our story, and we're sticking to it." He winked at Ava.

"If that's true, then maybe even I could fit in here," Ava said.

Jack did not smile at that. "You will, Ava. Just wait and see."

Ava thought she might cry. She had never thought of herself as the crying type, but since arriving in Pie Town, she'd nearly wept on a few occasions. To keep her eyes from leaking in front of Jack, she grabbed a glass of water and gulped it down.

Jack swallowed the last of his rum and got up to put on some music. "You like Bob Marley?" He stood near the back wall of the cafe, where a turntable rested on a console laden with albums.

"Doesn't everybody?" Ava replied.

The music and lyrics of "Three Little Birds" filled the space, but the volume was soft. Jack sang along as he Rasta danced his way back to the table. "'Don't worry 'bout a thing, cause every little thing gonna be all right.'"

As he sat down, Ava met his eyes. They were honest eyes, she thought, and kind. They were a pale shade of blue, more sky than sea. She found herself wanting to confide in him, which was also unlike her. She said, "This is a stranger place than I have ever been. But I like it here, and I'm not ready to leave. The people here seem even harder to understand than is usual for me. They won't answer most of my questions, at least not directly, but they keep giving me free stuff. So far, I haven't paid for any of my food since I arrived. The pies are especially good. I've eaten a shocking amount of pie."

Jack laughed at her look of astonishment, as Ava privately tallied up her pie consumption.

"That's to be expected. We're famous for our pie, and we like people to enjoy the other foods we serve too. I think you should try a huge slice of Annie's orange angel food cake."

"I won't say no because that would be rude, right?" Ava took the plate he passed her.

"Absolutely. Unforgivably rude," Jack answered. He poured another drink for himself and refilled Ava's hot chocolate.

Ava looked up between mouthfuls of cake long enough to ask, "What did you want to see me about?"

"I could say that I wanted to know how you are settling in, and that would be true. So, let's start there."

"Settling in? Is that what I'm doing?" Ava set down her fork, startled by the ring of truth in Jack's choice of words. "I was on my way back home to L.A. and ended up here on a whim. I intended to stay one night, but I changed my mind this morning. I figured I could stay for a week, get to know the town, and try to earn money to get back to L.A. without hitching rides."

Jack nodded. "A whim, was it?"

Ava tilted her head and looked off into the distance, squinting her eyes like someone with a migraine. She searched her mind for the remnants of a dream: a dream she'd had in Burke's truck, just before she said she wanted out. All she could recall with certainty was a town, off in the distance, beckoning her.

"You okay, Ava?"

She rubbed her eyes and refocused on Jack. "Something like a whim, anyway."

"Life can take us by surprise sometimes, can't it?"

"That's for sure."

"I'm glad to hear you're looking for work because I want to offer you a job. That's the main reason I was looking for you. I thought you seemed low on funds when I saw you yesterday. I knew you were still around because folks talk."

"Is that how you learned my name?" Ava asked.

Jack smiled. "That's a bit complicated, to tell you the truth. We all know your name, Ava, so don't feel like a stranger here."

Ava saw herself leaning over Harvey, looking at the cameo on his scarf and asking, *"Where'd your mama bird and her chicks fly off to, Harvey?"* She shuddered at the memory but couldn't have said why. Nor did she know why everyone she'd come across in this town seemed to know her name without her having once introduced herself. Angie flashed through her mind. *"Ava, this is not your story,"* she'd said. What could that mean? If a film about her mother giving birth to her was not her story, whose could it possibly be?

Maybe the amateur sci-fi mashup was the birthday surprise Evelyn had mentioned? But how could that be? It would have taken some time to make that movie, and she'd not told anyone she was coming here because she hadn't known herself. Besides, how would Evelyn have access to private footage of Jeannie? Ava reminded herself that someone, some unknown person, had been with her mom on Catalina Island and had filmed their adventure.

Could it be that she and Evelyn shared a father, the man Ava had never met and about whom Jeannie never spoke? Was that possible? Was it true that Evelyn could read her thoughts, or was it just a trick? Evelyn's face and voice crowded Ava's mind like a giant talking head that had come home to roost: *"I'm your next of kin . . . Like a sister . . . Born during an earthquake . . . It's our birthday . . . Twenty-one . . . Your home . . . What else could it be?"*

"Ava, are you sure you're okay?" Jack asked. It occurred to Ava that this seemed a natural role for him, one in which he was simultaneously overseer, advisor, and comforter.

Ava slapped her cheeks lightly with the palms of her hands. "Sorry. I keep spacing out, and I'm not sure why. I'm not normally like this. I guess I'm overwhelmed. So many things here are different from what I'm used to."

"Would it help you to know that confusion, forgetfulness, and spacing out are not unusual for newcomers to our area? Pie Town takes significant personal adjustment, and the orientation period can't be rushed. It's a highly individualized experience, but with some features common to most folks. People settle in at their own pace."

Ava nodded. Evelyn had told her much the same thing, but it felt reassuring to hear Jack repeat it. "Okay then, Jack, what can you tell me about cell phones? This guy I hitched a ride with gave me one, and I think I tried to call my mom. I can't remember making any calls, but that's what the phone log recorded. I can't get it to work now, though. Supposedly, there's Wi-Fi at the RV park, but I've not seen a single phone, phone tower, or computer anywhere in town."

"That's right. We are not a techno-savvy town, and that Wi-Fi sign mystifies all of us. No one remembers putting it up, but we've grown used to it being there and rarely notice it these days."

"Who owns the RV park?" Ava asked.

"Everybody," Jack replied, and then laughed. "Or nobody, depending on how you look at it. There used to be a couple who ran it, but they were not from around here."

"Where'd they come from?" Ava asked.

"A galaxy far, far away."

Ava laughed then and wondered why Jack didn't. Despite her habit of missing jokes, Ava could recognize a *Star Wars* quote when she heard one.

"They came as tourists and stayed a good while. They set up the RV Park as a place to live and a courtesy to other tourists. It went real well until the travel bug hit them again. Then, off they went—"

"—On an indefinite holiday?" Ava reached for the hot chocolate and poured the last of it into her mug.

"You want more angel food cake?" Jack asked, slicing himself a piece.

"No, thanks, I'm good."

"It was not an indefinite holiday, in the case of the Borgonthatchersleesdemains. We had a big party, and they said their goodbyes. I doubt we'll be seeing them again."

"Borgon . . . " Ava attempted the name but got lost two syllables in.

"Borgonthatcherleesdemains: that's their family name. Like I said, not from around here." Jack winked, and Ava laughed. "They were nice folks and popular around town. Ever since they left, the RV park has become a community project. We all contribute something to its upkeep, but it's light work; not many visitors stay there."

"I sure do like it," Ava said.

"I'm glad to hear that," Jack replied. "Now, let's get back to your question about communications. Everything I know about internet technology, I learned from visitors, like you, who came to town bearing phones and laptops. From what they have told me, connectivity here is random, sporadic and—in the final analysis—bizarre."

"Bizarre in what way, specifically?"

"I'm not sure I can say, specifically. I've thought a lot about this, and the best sense I can make of it is that the town itself must be providing the service whenever, however, and to whomever it wants. Of course, I can't be sure of that, but I am sure of this: Pie Town has no telecommunications companies, or services, or supporting infrastructure."

"Seriously? I thought I must be missing them, or that they were tucked away somewhere."

"No, you are not missing them. They don't exist. Seriously."

"Wow," Ava replied. "I don't use cell phones or computers myself, usually, but even I know that's impossible."

Jack nodded. "Indeed. My point is that your experience with your phone is not unique. Unfortunately, that's all I can confirm for you. I cannot explain about the call that you either did or did not make to your mother."

Ava nodded. She tucked her feet up into her roomy rattan armchair and listened to its creaking. She noticed the cafe had become much darker since she and Jack had begun talking. He had turned off most of the kitchen's overhead lights and blown out the candles. The two of them sat in overlapping pools of light provided by the Planet lamps near their table.

"The music stopped," she said, suddenly aware of the deepening silence. The record player had finished Bob Marley's *Exodus* album and then switched itself off.

"Yes, it's done for the night," Jack answered. He began stacking the plates on the table and brushing up cake crumbs with a napkin. "I've usually gone home to Annie and Lola by now."

"Sorry, am I keeping you?"

"Yep," Jack answered, then gave her a big smile, "But that's just fine. I invited you, remember?"

Ava liked how easily and naturally he smiled. In some ways, he reminded her of Jeannie.

"I remember," she replied and began helping him pile dishes and cutlery onto the tray.

Jack passed her the tray while he wiped down the table with a damp cloth, and the two of them walked into the kitchen.

"Look, Jack, I hope it's okay that I'm still at the camper. I'll look for somewhere else to stay if I need to."

"You stay there as long as you like, Ava." He passed her a clean towel and began washing the dishes, while Ava dried them. "Nobody else is going to be needing that camper anytime soon."

Ava felt inexplicably thrilled to hear this and marveled at how quickly she'd come to think of the Airstream as her home. "Should I keep leaving money in the drawer, or somewhere else? I don't think anyone ever collects it. There's money in there from two years ago."

Jack glanced sideways at her. "I know this will sound unbelievable, but money is unnecessary while you're here. You keep your cash."

Ava hung the dried mugs on cup hooks and then leaned against the counter with her arms folded. She watched Jack wiping down the sink. "Why are you so kind to me?" she asked.

Jack hung up his cloth and gestured for Ava to follow him as he completed the last of his closing duties. "Right off the top of my head, there are three reasons for my startling generosity. One is that you joined me here to partake of our leftovers, which feels a damn sight better than throwing fresh sandwiches and cakes into the bin. Two is that you are sleeping in Lenie and Rachel's Airstream, which causes me no disruption whatsoever. And three is that, if you were my kid and down on your luck, I'd hope somebody would give you a hand. All of that is why; is it enough?"

"More than enough, and thank you."

They ended up back at the table where they'd eaten and talked. Jack switched off the lamp closest to his chair and gestured at Ava to do the same. After locking up, they continued their conversation out on the sidewalk, by the light of a nearly-full moon. Ava glanced up just to be sure the candy-colored spaceships were still flying and then turned to face Jack, who was also looking up at the sky.

"It never gets old, seeing those ships," he said.

Ava's mind was on other things. She stuffed her hands into her jean pockets and took a deep breath. "Jack, you mentioned a job, which would be great. But I should tell you upfront that I'm not always good with people. I frequently misunderstand them and just as frequently say the wrong things, at the wrong times; or, so they tell me—the ones who are still speaking to me, that is."

Jack turned to face her. "Never mind people, Ava," he answered. "You like dogs?"

"I love dogs! And birds! And cats too!"

Her excitement startled Jack, who laughed. "Ava, that's got to be the most enthusiastic and heartfelt reply I've ever heard to that question." Turning toward the direction of the RV park, Jack said, "Come on. I'll walk you home. We live nearby. Our house is right across the street from the grocery store. You've probably seen it: it's got a bright orange door and a flock of pink plastic flamingoes in the front yard."

"I have seen it," Ava replied. "I noticed the flamingoes. I like all birds, even ones made of plastic and paper." She thought back to her missing origami crane, wondering if it would reappear as magically as it had disappeared.

"Now, about the job," Jack said. "Annie and I don't have kids, except for one very spoiled Irish setter. That's our Lola. She could use a playmate. As you may have noticed, there are no other dogs around here for her to run with, and Annie and I can't keep up with her."

They stopped walking when they reached the *Pie Town Gazette* office, at the end of the block where Ava would turn left to reach the RV park. "You see," Jack continued, "we used to travel a lot, the three of us. We weren't in Pie Town all the time. But that's a whole other story. Once we moved here permanently, we started opening the cafe a lot more often than we used to. Lola gets bored, and she's overfed due to customers sneaking her handouts. I thought maybe you'd like to take her out for an hour or two each day and show her a good time. We'd pay you, of course. How does that sound? Good deal?"

Jack thrust out his hand in a playful gesture, and Ava shook it. "That sounds awesome, Jack."

"Come by the cafe tomorrow, whenever you're ready, and I'll have Lola ready for you." He waved and headed toward home, before turning back. Ava was halfway down the alley already. "Ava, wait! You haven't asked about the salary yet."

"Whatever it is, I'll take it," Ava yelled over her shoulder. "Goodnight, Jack! And thank you!"

Thirteen

Fifth-grade Ava sat on the gym bleachers with her head bowed over her hands, as her thumbs and forefingers manipulated a paper fortune teller that she'd folded herself. In the dream, grown-up Ava hovered invisibly nearby, watching her younger self and aware she was dreaming. She remembered this moment from her childhood: sitting next to Jesse during Phys Ed, the last class on the final day of fifth grade. She remembered making the origami oracle and writing destinations on the inside flaps: beach, movies, water park, Disneyland. Then she'd spent the rest of the day telling her classmates what they would be doing that summer, whether or not they cared to hear it. Most of them ignored her, but she was used to that.

Adult Ava observed silently as the child's blonde hair slipped past her ear and partly obscured her face. Leaning in toward the girl was a boy with tousled black hair. In that way that people can just know things in dreams, Ava knew that this child was her school friend, Jesse. The part of her mind that knew she was dreaming, though, protested that Jesse had not been a boy but a girl. She knew, although she hadn't been able to understand it then, that she'd had a crush on Jesse, who was outgoing and kind to her. Jesse had sat with Ava at lunch that day and asked to see the fortune teller.

The fortune teller itself didn't look quite right in the dream, either. The observing part of Ava remembered how pleased she'd been with her handiwork. She'd made it from loose-leaf notebook paper and used her colored markers to write the fortunes on the inner folds and decorate the outer flaps. The fortune teller in the dream was a familiar sherbet-orange, with light blue writing on its visible parts.

Ava noticed that her fifth-grade self was now looking down at her moving hands while simultaneously looking up at her adult self. This ghost version of the child had split off from the rest of her and decided to chat with the dreamer. *She can see me. She's staring right at me.*

"I could sense your presence from the beginning, you know," the ghost child said, but in an adult voice that sounded like Ava's own twenty-year-old self. Ava glanced at the other two children, who remained huddled together manipulating the fortune teller. They seemed to be the dream now, and the ghost girl like a narrator giving a dramatic aside in a school play. Ava could no longer hear the children chatting and laughing. She heard only the ghost.

"I didn't understand at first, and I used to talk to Mom about you until I got old enough to know better. She thought you were one of my imaginary friends and began to worry that the movies we watched made it hard for me to distinguish fantasy from reality. I calmed her down by clamming up."

Ava had only a vague sense of her own physical presence within the dream, but it was enough to feel herself gaping at the girl, who smiled back at her.

"Was it wrong of me to send you out on your own, Ava? You had as much of me as I could give you. You had our memories, which you made your own. That's how it should be."

Ava found her voice. "This is a dream."

"Well," the ghost child replied, "it is, and it isn't." Ava stared as the ghost merged once again with the young Ava on the bleachers. The girl stood up, and the bleachers disappeared along with the rest of the gym and everyone in it.

Ava watched as her dream-child self morphed into an adult. "Don't forget we're in the dreamscape," Dream Self said to Sleeping Self. "I'm close enough now that I was able to connect with you through a dream. I used one of our shared memories because I thought it would be easier for you that way."

It was at that moment, precisely, that Ava's mind snapped to attention and screamed: *This isn't me!* She began struggling to surface from sleep but her dream twin, like a lovesick mermaid, kept tugging her under. Eventually, Ava foundered from the effort. She watched as her double unfolded one corner of the paper oracle and held it up for Ava to see. It said *remember* on one side and *miss you* on the other. The opposite corner of the paper had twisted itself into the head of a bird, which winked at her.

"Who *are* you?" Ava woke herself up in a panic, half-shouting the question. She was not surprised to find that she'd dozed off on the red leatherette couch, or that her thoughts were zipping around like manic Marvin's tiny spaceship again.

Another Evelyn. Another Evelyn. Another Evelyn.

Ava jumped up from the couch and began rummaging through the camper, hoping to find the sherbet-orange crane, but it remained mysteriously AWOL. Running out of places to search, she rinsed her face with cold water and put the kettle on to boil. As she sipped coffee, she reminded herself that she had a job now and, even better, a sense of belonging that she hadn't felt since she didn't know when; maybe never.

Everything's fine. A stupid dream, that's all. The paper crane will turn up eventually.

Deciding the day would begin with bluebirds and happiness, Ava slipped into a short white cotton skirt and topped it off with a pale-yellow t-shirt featuring a pair of plump western bluebirds. Ropey summer sandals completed the look and made her wonder, fleetingly, what season was happening outside of Pie Town. Brushing her hair in the mirror, she noticed that the internal current that she'd grown used to, and even come to like, was still humming along. She wondered whether it a town-sponsored healing technique, or if there were medicinal herbs baked into the pies that made her blood tingle and excited the hairs on her skin. She couldn't help but notice that, despite an uneasy night's sleep, she felt great. Today, she planned to enjoy breakfast at the diner and then pick up Lola at Cafe Z and take her to play; after that, she would drop in on Evelyn and ask her what she knew about the rejuvenating properties of Pie Town.

Ava sat at the booth which she already considered her regular place in the Flying Saucer Diner and watched Julie approaching her table. She was surprised when the waitress smiled at her.

"Good morning," Ava said.

"Good morning back to you. What would you like for breakfast?"

"Maybe something different today. I usually have an egg."

"How about pancakes? Sarah is on the griddle right now, and nobody flips better cakes than Sarah. Also, there's fresh berries and real maple syrup."

"Count me in, please," Ava replied.

Julie filled Ava's coffee cup and then looked at her. "Were you still wanting the guided tour?"

"Yes, thanks. Is the guide here today?"

"She's out back with the staff, loading up on pancakes. I'll let her know you're here."

Ava wondered if the guide would mind having a dog along. She was trying to decide whether she should fetch Lola when Jasmine walked out of the kitchen bearing a tray. Today, Jasmine was dressed differently from Julie, who had been wearing jeans with a white cotton shirt and an apron. Jasmine's dress was grasshopper green, and it was evident that she'd made it herself by sewing a pleated peplum around the waist of a scoop-necked nylon spandex tank top. The bottom of the tank extended a few inches lower than the peplum, forming a straight skirt that clung to her thighs and barely covered her backside. On her feet were a pair of chunky red ankle boots, and on her wrists, she wore silver cuffs. The highlight of the ensemble, Ava thought, was simply the girl herself: golden-brown skin with reddish undertones, bright green eyes, and shining black hair. Jasmine bounced over to Ava's table with a smile on her face. Ava set down her coffee, wary but interested.

"Hi!" Jasmine practically shouted at Ava, before plunking Ava's pancakes down and sliding into the booth. She looked at Ava from across the table. "You'll love those pancakes, trust me. Go ahead, dig in."

Ava poured syrup on her short stack of cakes and took a bite. "You're right; they're the best. As good as my mom's, I think." She'd not meant to start off talking about her mom, like a six-year-old.

"As soon as you're finished eating, we can go. You want the whole tour, right? And you've got a coupon from M(1a)?"

Ava reached into her backpack and pulled out the paper that had been slipped under her door yesterday, "Yes. Do you want to see it?" She passed it to Jasmine. I don't know

M(1a). I've never met him, but you're the second person who's mentioned him to me."

Jasmine looked at the coupon, nodded, and passed it back to Ava. "It's definitely from him. It's got the smell of his ditto machine all over it, and his signature, such as it is, printed at the bottom. It's a compliment getting one of those, you know. He rarely gives them out."

"Why would he give one to me, when he doesn't even know me?" Ava asked.

"You mean he is a stranger to you?"

"Yes. I don't know much about the Ms, but I've seen them here in the diner. They are the three gentlemen with the bowler caps, right?"

"Yes, that would be our town fathers, sure enough. But clearly, you are not a stranger to them, Ava." Jasmine looked at her in a way that Ava could not interpret, with her head cocked to one side and an inquisitive expression. Did she imagine that Ava was lying about not knowing them?

Ava cleared her throat. "What makes you say that?"

"Because you have the coupon," Jasmine replied. "Here, let me fix it up. Be right back." Before Ava could respond, Jasmine had snatched the coupon out of her hand and was rushing away with it. Ava decided to finish her pancakes while she was gone. They were too good to waste.

Jasmine bounced her way back to Ava's table from the back of the diner, reminding Ava of a sleek rabbit. She was more buoyant than Harvey and moved with nearly as much energy. The thought made Ava smile.

"What's funny?" Jasmine asked her, sliding into the booth again and pushing Ava's coupon back to her.

"Nothing, just . . . You seem different today from yesterday. I didn't think you liked me much yesterday. Of course, maybe you still don't—Oh, this is nice!" Ava held the warm, plasticized coupon in her hand, and then rubbed it against her cheek to feel the smooth, flexible glide of it.

"I laminated it," Jasmine announced. "Now, you can keep it in good shape so that it won't wear out. Those coupons are good forever. No expiration date."

"Thanks, Jasmine."

Ava slipped the coupon back into her pack, nestling it alongside the three Marys, and then looked up at the other girl, unsure of how to proceed with the conversation.

"About yesterday, Ava? Can we just start over?" Jasmine asked.

Ava let out her breath, which she had not known she was holding. "Absolutely we can. I'm glad to hear you say that."

"When you rocked into town, I had been busy all afternoon unpacking deliveries. I didn't know you were coming. The word might have got around town but not to Jack or me. He'd been at a catering gig. Jack isn't like me, though. He just takes everything in stride, you know? Always the big old pussycat who got the cream, our Jack. The cream being Annie, of course," Jasmine said, snorting as she laughed at her joke.

Ava was silent.

"So, one minute I'm working in my shop and the next thing I know, there you are! We like to prepare ourselves for incomers because they can destabilize our town and our lives—which amounts to the same thing. Anyway, I panicked because I thought there'd been a border breach, possibly through my building. I didn't realize you'd been invited, and I wholeheartedly apologize for freaking out like that."

Jasmine was looking at her expectantly, but Ava was not sure what she wanted her to say. *What's a border breach?* She longed for a morning free of difficult discussions, so she decided to go with a familiar topic that she'd already covered with Evelyn and Jack.

"Thanks for the apology, but I didn't realize I'd been invited, either, Jasmine. I just saw the town in the distance, off the highway, and wanted to stay a night. That's all."

"I was rude to you. I won't pretend that's totally out of character for me, but I do grow on people after a while, usually." Jasmine stopped speaking and reached out to grasp Ava's left hand, which lay on the table between them. She smiled encouragingly and said, "I'm glad you're here now, though. We all are."

Ava sat staring at her, with her eyes wide open and her mouth slightly agape, forgetting to be self-conscious.

"What difference did you believe my arrival would make, Jasmine? I'm nobody special. Just another tourist. From what I hear, people come in droves just to eat pie."

"Ava, your specialness has its own story, which is not mine to tell." Jasmine sighed.

Ava looked at their hands, clasped on the table. *Jasmine is holding my hand*, she thought, and immediately wished she hadn't, because the moment the astonishment of physical contact distracted her from Jasmine's words, she felt herself blushing head-to-toe. Jasmine released Ava's hand and sat back, still smiling and looking completely at ease.

"People here say that a lot," Ava said. "They talk about stories, and stories within stories, and whose stories they are to understand or not to understand, to tell or not to tell. They tend to avoid answering direct questions with direct answers. Jack has helped me, though.

"I've seen and heard some pretty crazy things from one of your locals, including personal things about my family that I don't know how she knows. I assume that she means well . . ." Ava stopped. She didn't want to talk about Evelyn yet, whose kinship she was beginning to take seriously based on their conspicuous genetic link, but whose mental stability and trustworthiness worried her.

"Look, can we just go for a walk now? Do you mind giving me the tour?" Ava figured she should ask, as it dawned on her that Jasmine might have been sitting with her because it was part of her job as a tour guide to be hospitable, and not because she liked her and wanted to spend time together.

"Ava, I would be delighted to give you a tour. Even more, I would love to make you dinner tonight at my place, if you're free?" She gave Ava a smile that left no room for misunderstanding, even for someone prone to it.

"You have the most beautiful skin I've ever seen," Ava replied, and then added, "I hope that's okay to say. I mean, seriously, you are so unlike anyone I've ever known."

"I don't doubt that my skin, at least, is unlike anyone you've ever known. The color combination is unique to Julie and me. It's a cream and titanium base with some mixture of walnut brown, raw umber, and burnt ochre finished with a rub of Pompeian red, or possibly Venetian. The rubbing is what gives it that burnished look. That's how Rachel explained it to me." Jasmine paused and bowed her head, touching her right palm briefly to her chest, just as Ava had seen Evelyn do back at the motel, whenever she mentioned Rachel and Lenie. Jack, though, had not done this. He'd spoken of the two women in a friendly but non-reverential tone, as one might speak of one's friends.

"I'm no artist, just a shopkeeper," Jasmine continued, "so I don't know much about the subtleties of light and color, and Rachel couldn't remember specifically what she'd used. She had to guess from examining the drawings. They'd been stuck in her notebook a long time, though, so they'd been exposed to the aging and decay of the outer desert. Once we dismantled the notebook and displayed the drawings, the town began restoring them to their original condition. They are becoming clearer and more vibrant all the time. Anyway, I am glad you admire my flesh tones, Ava. Thanks for saying so."

"You're welcome," Ava replied. It was all she could think of to say.

Fourteen

As they stepped out of the diner onto the sidewalk, Jasmine hooked her arm through Ava's and pointed out the buildings as they walked.

"Next to the diner, we have the Galaxy Department Store and Sol's Drugs and More. They're connected inside, and Sandy manages both places with a small staff. Sandy owns the department store, and Sol owns the drugstore, but Sol spends most of his time at the visitor center, where he has another store.

Next to the shops, we have Skylights Park. Let's take a stroll."

Jasmine led her into the park where Ava had first met Harvey. Jasmine gathered a handful of perky daisies that were growing under the eucalyptus trees and passed the bouquet to Ava.

"Thanks, they're lovely."

"Press them in a book and see what happens."

Ava's eyes grew wide as she looked at Jasmine. "Seriously? What happens?"

"You end up with flat daisies," Jasmine replied.

Ava laughed, happy to have caught the joke. They wandered out of the park and back onto the sidewalk, continuing the tour on the next block.

"On the corner, we have Cafe Z, which belongs to Jack and Annie. They're both excellent cooks, and everybody loves them. Two doors down from their place is Cinema Retrograde, and that's Rocket Records between the two. Suzy is the owner of Rocket, and her stock is first-rate. Unfortunately, we can't play the records anywhere in town except in the shop or Cafe Z, because they're the only two places with turntables and speakers. The diner has a jukebox, but that's it for music in Pie Town. We've been trying to change this for a long time, but the town interferes. It seems to have firm ideas about where music does and does not belong, and what records are okay to play."

"Jasmine, what do you mean by 'the town interferes'?"

"We have replicated turntables and speakers on several occasions. There's a quartet made up of Sol, Sid, Evelyn, and Angie—I know you've not met all of them yet, but you will—that meets regularly to draw up plans and implement them. They build custom items by request, which are unavailable through our off-world vendors. Unfortunately, the record players disappear in a flash whenever we attempt to use them."

"Disappear? Literally?"

"Sure thing. The three Ms are negotiating with the town now, on our behalf, so we'll see what happens next."

"Wow," Ava replied.

"Yeah, that kind of thing probably doesn't happen where you come from, right?"

Ava shook her head. "No. Our cities and towns aren't . . ."

"Aren't?" Jasmine prompted.

Ava shook her head again and said, "Never mind."

They resumed walking to the end of the sidewalk, where the deserted-looking motel's white stucco walls shone in the sunlight.

"Hey, Jasmine? Do you know Harvey?"

"Sure thing. Harvey drops by my store a lot, and we sometimes hang out at the diner together. Harvey's a favorite with those of us lucky enough to see him."

Ava thought about Jack saying that he hadn't met Harvey. "Not everyone can see him?"

"That's right. Harvey is shy, and it takes him a long time to reveal himself, especially to men. He prefers women but will befriend men if he trusts them. Of course, the three Ms are the exception to his women-only rule, just as they are the exception to nearly every rule in Pie Town."

"Jack doesn't know Harvey," Ava said. "Why wouldn't Harvey trust Jack?"

"It's not Jack. Harvey tries to avoid Lola because she's highly energetic and playful. Harvey likes peace and quiet. He gets overstimulated easily."

"Like me."

Jasmine laughed. "Yes, that's probably why he likes you so much. There's a natural affinity."

"He said he liked me?"

"He did," Jasmine replied. "Just this morning. He mentioned too that you've already visited the motel here at the edge of town, where he lives, along with Evelyn and Beau and a few others."

Ava nodded, wondering if Beau was the guy who'd stuck his head out of a bungalow door and waved. "Yes, I met Evelyn. We spent yesterday afternoon together, at her invitation."

Jasmine nodded but did not comment or ask Ava if she wanted to drop in to visit Evelyn. Instead, she took Ava's hand in hers and led her across the street, where they stopped in front of the church with the bell tower.

"Here's our gracious adobe chapel. As you've probably noticed, it looks way older than everything else. We know it preceded the town, but we don't know by how many suns and moons."

"The exterior architecture is seventeenth-century Spanish colonial mission," Ava explained.

Jasmine stepped back and dropped Ava's hand. "Wow, listen to you! You know about those kinds of things?

"No, not much, only what my mother has told me over the years. She's interested in the architecture of the Americas, and she's an amateur interior designer. She works for a design firm, in administration. Anyway, we have chapels like this where I come from."

"Well, there aren't any events scheduled right now, but it's always open if you want to go inside. Shall we have a look?"

Ava hesitated. She did want to look inside, but a feeling of foreboding stopped her. Instead of responding to Jasmine's question, she stood at the top of the chapel stairs, squinting up at the bell tower.

She must have stared for too long because Jasmine startled her by shaking her arm and asking, "Hey, Ava? Are you all right?

Ava nodded. "Yeah, sorry. I'm all right, but I don't feel like going inside just now."

"That's okay, let's keep walking."

Jasmine linked their arms again, and they continued.

"Next to the chapel are some of our houses," Jasmine said. As the two of them walked around the block, Ava counted eight tidy, ranch-style houses which faced the street but backed onto a shared garden. The houses looked very much like the ones she'd noticed this morning, on her way to the diner: modest but attractive mid-century modern ranch houses.

"Are all the houses like this? This style, I mean?"

"Yes, they don't vary much. There are seven designs and twenty-one houses in town, spread over three blocks; so, none of the blocks has a duplicate house on it."

"Which is more than you can say for the people," Ava said.

Jasmine stopped and turned to Ava. "That's true. Does it disturb you? I guess that's not common, either, where you come from."

"Disturb me?" Ava considered this before speaking. "I've never come across multiple sets of twins and triplets anywhere else. I've been here only a little while, and this is a small town. I admit that it puzzles me, but it doesn't disturb me."

"We are an unusual place, Ava, in more ways than one."

"Yes, and I'm still learning. I'm not bothered by people looking alike, as long as I can tell who's who," Ava answered, trying not to think about her own lookalike. "And I believe I can tell you apart, at least when it comes to you and Julie."

Jasmine's face lit up. "You have no trouble telling the two of us apart? I wonder why that would be?"

Ava felt herself turning what must have been a thousand shades of red and stammered, "What were you saying about the houses?"

Jasmine laughed and resumed walking. "The houses you see have always been here, and we wouldn't recognize our town without them. We'd feel insulted if other types of houses sprung up without our approval."

"Has that ever happened?" Ava asked. "Houses just springing up?"

"Once, yes. That's a whole other long story which I'll tell you sometime." Jasmine led her toward the block where Ava was staying.

"On this block, of course, you know all about the Infinite Express RV Park. In front of that, we have the town hall; the municipal offices building, which houses our library; and the *Pie Town Gazette* office. The town fathers look after those."

They kept walking until they were at the corner of Jasmine's block, where her grocery store was located and where the town effectively came to an end. They passed by the Infinite Express Filler Up, which Jasmine said was owned by nobody but itself and functioned automatically.

"How does that work?" Ava asked, fascinated.

"How does anything work? It's machine-operated, and there's a robot who keeps it clean, answers questions, and resolves problems.

"A robot? Wow, can I meet him? Or her?"

"It's not that kind of robot. You're thinking I mean like something out of one of the sci-fi movies we have at the cinema. It's not 'him' or 'her.' It has no body or personal identity, as far as we can tell. Let's say you walk into the shop, and you can't find your favorite chocolate bar, or you want some oil for your crankshaft."

"What's a crankshaft?"

"I don't know, something to do with an engine. I heard it in a movie once. Anyway, what you do is you say 'Hello, Filler Up, would you tell me where to find a crankshaft and a Supernova Chocolate Bar?' and it answers you from speakers installed in the ceiling."

"Far out."

"Yep."

"Jasmine?" Ava stopped walking, and Jasmine glanced up at her. "I've never seen any cars here."

"You mean motor cars like people drive in the movies?"

Ava nodded.

"We don't have those, not real ones anyway. The gas-guzzlers we have, which you will see parked behind the diner and maybe other places around town, are not what they appear to be."

"What are they? And what do you need a Filler Up for?"

Jasmine ignored the first question but answered the second.

"The Infinite Express Filler Up is a joint venture between the town and the superhighway. It used to be staffed by locals, but we all prefer it as it is now. The whole story involving the town and the highway is complicated and maybe too much to go into right now. Trust me on this, okay?"

Ava nodded, relieved. She didn't want to be complicated right now, either. She just wanted to enjoy Jasmine's company and rest her mind for a while. The two of them stood in front of the Luna Bar & Grill, which looked closed.

"The Luna opens and closes on a whim because the owners both have jobs at the visitor center, which keeps them busy. Anyway, the Baxters throw parties for us townies now and again. We eat and play games and tell stories. There's no music, of course."

"The Baxters?"

"They're the owners: Baxter and Baxter. Two fellows who look as alike as Julie and me but who are a couple.

They've been together for as long as I've known them. They're sweet guys."

Ava smiled. "Can you tell them apart?"

"Those of us who arrived in town with them can, yes, even though the differences are subtle."

Ava waited for Jasmine to disclose the secret of discerning one Baxter from the other, but it wasn't forthcoming. Jasmine pulled Ava down the block until they reached Zoom-the-Moon, her grocery store.

"There are more houses out the back of us." Jasmine gestured toward the two-thirds of her block that extended behind the grocery, the gas station, and the bar, which contained four houses and a central garden. "If you look across the street, you can see houses are taking up that block too. The town consists of eight blocks, three of which have houses on them. All of the houses face either the main street, or an alley, or the desert, and all of them back onto their block's shared garden."

"What about the visitor center Jack told me about?" Ava asked. "And where is the Infinite Loop? I've seen the signs for it."

"You will see those when the time is right," Jasmine answered, "which isn't yet."

Ava thought she could make a long and detailed list of things that people in Pie Town said to her that made absolutely no sense. She realized, too, that Jasmine had shown her nothing that she had not already seen. She wondered why she'd needed a coupon for the tour.

"That's pretty much it. Home, sweet home. Is there anything you'd like a closer look at? I don't like to give canned tours—people end up getting a little bit of everything and not enough of what they truly want." She winked at Ava, who felt the blood rush to her cheeks again.

"Maybe we could take a closer look at the gardens?" Ava asked, and then remembered her most important errand of the day. "Jasmine, I'm supposed to be walking Jack and Annie's dog, Lola. Do you think we could go back to the cafe and pick her up?"

"Of course we can!" Jasmine grabbed Ava's hand and trotted down the street with her in tow. It was like keeping up with Harvey, only harder in two-inch wedge heels.

Lola was waiting at the door of Cafe Z with a ball in her mouth and bounded out to greet the girls when they approached. They crossed the street to the block of houses next to the chapel, entering a lush rose garden bursting its bounds with several varieties of pink and cream flowers. The proud centerpiece was a white trellis arch covered in perfect, crimson-velvet blooms. As they walked, Lola stopped to sniff everything, while Ava pointed out the roses she recognized.

"You know roses date back to ancient China and Greece and even show up in the Egyptian pyramids?"

"Mummified?"

"No, in paintings," Ava replied. She knew she was showing off but couldn't help wanting to impress Jasmine. "It's surprising that they'll grow here. After all, we are in the desert even if it doesn't feel like it. Egypt wasn't always a desert, you know."

"Yes," replied Jasmine "this is a very special place, as I'm sure you've noticed. The weather is pretty much the same every day, but we have underground springs that feed the plants and provide our water."

They followed Lola's lead to the garden at the center of the block nearest the diner. This one was more what Ava would have expected: plentiful native desert plants, like those in Skylights Park. They continued to the garden behind

Jasmine's grocery, and Ava was pleased to find it contained herbs and leafy greens encircling a stand of sunflowers.

"Is this one yours?"

"They belong to all of us," Jasmine said, "but this one is my favorite."

"It reminds me of you."

"More than the prickly pear in the other garden?" Jasmine shot back with a laugh. Ava wanted to say that a basil plant was better than a cactus, or even a rose, but she couldn't find the right words, so she changed the subject.

"You referred to the little houses as 'ours'? Do you live in one of them?"

"I could. One of the houses is mine, but I prefer the apartment over my store. Better view and more interesting. If you come for dinner tonight, I'll show you."

Ava felt herself blushing again but managed to say that she'd love to come for dinner.

"The town tour is a chance for you to connect with a local person and get oriented, but it's not that useful when you've already been here a couple of days, and there's simply no way to rush the slow revelation of our landmarks. Most of the townsfolk, during the day, work over at the visitor center, if you're wondering why you don't see them around much. It's huge and thriving, with traffic in and out all day, and a busy hotel where most of the tourists stay. Had you wondered why our street is so quiet in the daytime?"

Ava nodded. She had wondered but didn't want to admit that she'd been worried about people avoiding her, after her first blast of rejection from Jasmine. "I had, yes, because I noticed the town is livelier after dark."

"Sure thing. Anyway, the real tour is the one that you need the coupon for, and that happens at my place."

Ava glanced at Jasmine, to see if there was a joke in there somewhere that she was missing.

"Seriously? The coupon is for a private tour of your apartment?"

Jasmine laughed. "Yes, it is. Sounds weird, right? That's why I am the only one who gives that tour, and few visitors get invited. That should let you know that you are someone special to us, Ava." She caught Ava's eye then and smiled warmly. "I would have invited you home myself, even without the coupon."

Ava felt tears welling in her eyes. She stared at her sandals, hoping that Jasmine wouldn't notice. "Thank you," she said.

She felt Jasmine brush a hand across her left cheek, but she didn't look up.

"Sure thing," Jasmine replied, softly. "I suppose I'd better open up the store for a while in case anyone needs emergency supplies, like economy bags of corn chips, canned orange drink, and off-brand bean dip." Ava glanced up then, and Jasmine winked at her, flashing a brilliant smile.

Boop-Oop-a-Doop! ran through Ava's mind again, but she stayed silent, afraid of ruining the moment. Jasmine reached down to scruffle Lola's head and then was waving goodbye to them both before Ava could think of what to say. "Come to dinner at twilight!" Jasmine called over her shoulder.

Ava decided to skip her visit to Evelyn and keep Lola a while longer. She took the dog over to the RV park, where Lola fetched her ball from the pool over and over until they were both tired out. Afterward, Ava dozed on a lounger while Lola lay next to her, dreaming and woofing in her sleep. The RV park was quiet but for the two of them and the occasional lapping of pool water when the gentle wind moved across it. Lola's wet tongue on her hand woke Ava with a start.

"I'd better get you back," she told the dog, who answered by tilting her head to the right.

"Does it feel way past lunchtime to you?"

Lola tilted her head to the left.

"I don't want to eat too close to dinner time, but I don't want to show up starving either. You know?"

Right head tilt.

"Being human is hard."

Left tilt, followed by a gentle moan.

Ava let herself into Cafe Z, prepared to apologize for keeping Lola out so long, but Jack greeted her with a hearty, "Perfect timing. Here, sample these." He set a tray of bite-sized tarts on the closest table. "It's a new recipe, and I need an opinion. I'll get you some iced tea to go with them." He gave Lola a good scratch behind the ears and then disappeared into the kitchen.

Ava was hungry and decided that the polite thing to do was sit down and eat. Lola settled on the floor next to her, and Ava fed her several of the little tarts. Ava had just popped a fifth tart into her own mouth when Jack reappeared with two glasses of tea and a bowl of water. He set the water down near Lola before sitting down at the table. Ava nodded at him and mumbled "*Mmmmmm!*" as she chewed.

"I was thinking of calling them 'mini crab & cheddar quiches' on the menu, but that makes it sound like baby crabs are involved. Not a good visual. I believe they need a splash of truffle oil too. I'll try that on the next batch."

"Let me see," Ava said. There were two tarts left on the plate. She gave one to Lola and ate the last one herself. After they'd both swallowed, Ava offered her critique. "We don't see how they could be any better."

"Thanks. If you're still hungry, I could make you a crab salad roll. I have leftover crab."

Ava glanced toward the windows to see if the sun was setting, but the curtains were drawn. "I'm not sure how long Lola and I slept by the pool. Do you think it will be dark soon?" Jasmine had told her to come to her place at twilight because, Ava mused, that's how you tell time without clocks. "I have dinner plans. I'm supposed to be at Jasmine's place around nightfall, but I need to freshen up first."

Jack nodded and scratched Lola's head, which she was resting against his leg. "You'd better be off then because it's nearly dusk. I'm sure you've noticed we don't worry too much about precision timing here, but Lola and I don't want to make you late for dinner."

Fifteen

Ava left Cafe Z and headed for the camper, where she stopped to have a quick shower and change into jeans and her favorite raven t-shirt. She walked up the alley and around the corner to Jasmine's shop, where she saw that Zoom-the-Moon's neon sign was switched off and the shop's interior dark. Following Jasmine's instructions, she continued around the back of the building and entered through the staff door, which led into an industrial-gray foyer. There was a matching gray metal door on her right that said "Stockroom" and nothing on her left except a red letter box mounted on the wall. The only decorative touch appeared on the wall to her left: stenciled blackbirds, repeated dozens of times to simulate ascent. Ava saw that their flight followed the angle of the metal stairs to the top, and then turned and continued upward beyond the first landing. She guessed the blackbirds would fly her all the way to Jasmine, and this brought an unconscious smile to her lips.

The building was narrow, and its ground-floor ceiling high, making for a steep stair climb. Straight in front of her was the first flight, which she ascended before turning right at a landing and heading up another flight, to another landing, and then ascending another flight, to yet another landing. By time Ava reached Jasmine's glossy red door, which matched the letter box, she'd lost count of the flights and was out of breath. She'd seen no other doors or hallways on her way up and was annoyed at herself for losing count. Nevertheless, she didn't want to go back down and start over. The blackbird motif ended on the door, where a single bird came to rest on a black twig painted below the brass knocker.

Ava had her hand poised on the knocker when Jasmine threw open the door and beamed at her. She was wearing the jeans and white shirt that Ava knew she wore for work, but without the polka-dot scarf, and she was padding around barefoot. Ava froze. This was exactly the kind of situation that she hated. Should she take her shoes off, or would that look weird? She stood in the doorway unable to decide. Apparently unaware of her quandary, Jasmine pulled her across the threshold. Ava noticed two things then, simultaneously: one was her heart speeding up, and the other was that she felt ridiculous towering over Jasmine in her sandals when she was at least six inches taller in bare feet. That decided things for her. Ava paused and pulled off her shoes so that she could look at Jasmine without feeling like an adult looming over a child.

Jasmine gestured around the vast open space that was her apartment and said, "Welcome to my home, Ava. Please have a look around while I cook. I hope you're not starving because I just got going in the kitchen."

As Jasmine headed back to their dinner preparations, Ava moved to the middle of the immense room, where she stood still and silent, taking in its impossible geometry. She'd expected a small apartment, the type typically built over shops in narrow two- or three-story buildings. She'd thought it might have an industrial vibe because that's what she imagined would appeal to Jasmine. She found herself standing in an enormous rectangular room that reminded her of the Natural History Museum in Los Angeles. Though, instead of glassed-in exhibits lining the walls, there were doors. Ava counted them: there were nine on each long wall and three on each of the short walls. The apartment's floor space and the doors were softly lit by the kind of posh lighting that she had only ever seen in galleries and museums.

Some of the doors were metal, some were wood, and some were metal and wood. Most of the wood ones were painted in a rich shade of blue, red, green, black, or white. Others were unpainted and looked ancient, as if cut from primeval trees. Many of these old ones had designs engraved or carved into them: evocative faces, hands, and symbols. Ava wanted to run her hands over the carvings but felt unsure about touching them. *What if they touch back?* She glanced up at the second level of the apartment, which consisted of a wraparound balcony that stretched the entire length of each wall. She counted two dozen doors up there too.

Casting her eyes farther upward, Ava gasped. Instead of a solid ceiling, she was looking through glass panes, at least fifty feet overhead. She could see a clear night sky, splashed with shining stars and planets in a wide array of vivid colors: red, yellow, blue, orange, pink, violet. She blinked hard and looked again, but they were still there, and still as strangely colorful. She noticed what was missing too: zippy spaceships. She started to cross the room to look out and see how the town appeared from up here but held back. If the building's cavernous interior and assorted doors had not been enough to confound her utterly, the unexpected transformation of the galaxy's skyscape had done the job. Ava was tempted to go back outside and take another look at the building and its surrounds, from ground level.

Without meaning to speak aloud, she heard herself whispering, "Impossible." The room's acoustics were flawless, mimicking the properties of certain old castles and cathedrals. In the kitchen, Jasmine heard Ava's astonished whisper and was quickly at her side.

"I'm sorry, I probably should have warned you," Jasmine said with a grin. "But you should see the look on your face. You'd better blink before your eyes pop out."

Ava closed her eyes, running her hands over her face and through her hair.

"I did tell you it was interesting."

"Yes, you did," Ava answered quietly. She was trying to decide if she was safe. Everything felt unstable, like a world tilted on its axis. Everything except Jasmine.

"Seriously, though?" Jasmine continued, "Try not to freak out if you look out the window for a view of the town because you can't see it from here."

"I don't understand," Ava replied.

"Understanding is overrated, in my opinion. Just go with it, okay? For now, anyway. We can talk during dinner. In the meantime, don't forget to keep breathing in and out." Suddenly, Jasmine leaned closer and upwards toward Ava, planting a kiss on her cheek before Ava realized what was happening.

Ava laughed. "Thanks!"

"I'm glad you're here. Now, I hope you like vegetable pizza with loads of anchovies because that's what I'm making."

"It's my favorite." Ava felt herself relaxing and realized that, despite their prickly introduction, Jasmine's presence was beginning to have a calming effect on her. *Like Harvey does*, she thought, *or Lola*. Well, not exactly like those two. This relationship was different from her friendships with them, or she hoped it would be. Evelyn, on the other hand, made Ava feel keyed up. Ava felt guilty about this but could not seem to help it, and she found herself wanting to avoid Evelyn.

She gestured to the doors on the wall closest to her and asked Jasmine, "Where do they lead?"

Jasmine cocked her head at Ava, reminding Ava of Lola, "You're welcome to have a look. It's okay to peek, but don't cross the thresholds."

Ava reached out toward the nearest door, which was constructed of bronze metal and covered with cogs and gears.

"Wait, don't!" Jasmine said, but Ava had already pulled her hand away from the copper knob. "Sorry, not that one. If you open that one, you won't want to open any of the others." Ava stared at the polished metal door while backing away from it. She clasped her right hand in her left until it stopped shaking.

"What's behind there, Jasmine? My whole body feels electrified. Not in a bad way, but familiar. Is your apartment the reason I've felt like live current has been flowing through me ever since I got to Pie Town?"

"Sure thing," Jasmine said, beaming at Ava as though proud of the fact. "Ava, meet the Doors. They are unlike any other doors you will encounter in Pie Town, and you should approach them at all times with respect and caution. Don't worry, though. There's not a mega generator or nuclear power source behind any of them. What is there is odder and more esoteric than that but not dangerous in an electrical sense." She considered her words for a moment before continuing. "Though, some of them may be dangerous in other ways. Now, how about a drink? Cocktail, wine, soda, juice, sparkling water? I've got everything."

"Juice with fizzy water would be great, thanks." Ava watched Jasmine bounce toward the kitchen. She could see that Jasmine's real apartment—the kitchen, lounge area, study, storage cupboards, sleeping loft, and what she assumed to be an enclosed bathroom—resembled a stage set built into one corner of the extensive room. This living area had been partitioned off to create an aesthetically unified space, providing a sense of intimacy that would have been absent otherwise. In keeping with the town's preferred era, the decor was entirely mid-century modern.

Jasmine returned to Ava bearing iced drinks with lime slices and paper umbrellas. She passed one to her guest. "This is my house specialty. I don't drink much alcohol, myself, but I make tasty fruit concoctions. This punch is orange, cranberry, cactus, and wild lime with soda." Jasmine paused and raised her glass, "Welcome home, Ava."

Ava smiled and raised hers, too, feeling a lump in her throat. *Welcome home?* Did she mean that in the same way Evelyn had, or was she saying something else? Ava coughed out the one word she could manage, which was, fortunately, appropriate: "Cheers!"

Ava decided to wait for Jasmine before peeking behind any Doors. While Jasmine cooked, she wandered through the apartment. After walking around the borders of the lower level twice, keeping her distance from the windows, she took one of two spiral staircases up to the balcony. As she walked the perimeter, examining the intricate details on some of the Doors, she came across a large handle mounted on a cast iron base. The base was shaped like a hand, with the index finger pointing up. Discreet arrows indicated that right turns were for closing and left for opening.

"Your ceiling opens?" She called out to Jasmine, who was piling vegetables on top of pizza crusts at her kitchen island. Because Ava was on the balcony, the two could see each other over the partitions when Jasmine looked up. "Sure thing. We like to keep an eye on the universe, you know. I host star parties for the town regulars. The handle looks like hard work, but it's smooth and easy. You can try it if you like."

Ava reached for the handle, but a faint scratching sound behind her startled her. She turned to see what was there.

Nothing.

Ava began to turn the wood handle, which had a satisfying heft and a beautiful patina. It turned just as smoothly as Jasmine had said it would. As she turned the crank, the ceiling's glass panels separated into eight enormous pieces that extended fully outward, before fading like mist into the alien sky. Ava had never seen glass behave like that and thought it must be a sophisticated illusion. By the time she had turned the handle as far as she could, the apartment was wholly open to the opulent night.

"Jasmine, this is amazing," Ava called out, "even though I don't understand what I'm seeing. The planets are strange colors."

A voice answered her, but it was not Jasmine's. It was not human, either. But then again, was Jasmine? Ava wondered.

"*Meow*," the voice repeated. Ava turned to see a cat with a luxurious chocolate and cream coat pushing its way through a pet door at the base of one of the more modern-looking Doors, which was painted blue and had a satin chrome knob.

"Well, aren't you beautiful," she said to the cat, admiring its seal-point markings, white-mitten paws, and exceedingly bushy tail.

"There you are, Broussy! Good thing, I wanted Ava to meet you," Jasmine had slipped silently up the stairs and was standing next to Ava, dangling an anchovy from her right hand. The cat glanced up at Ava, who was startled by the intensity of its mismatched eyes: one bright green, the other bright blue.

"Ava, this is Broussard," Jasmine said. "Broussard, this is my friend Ava." Broussard rubbed against Jasmine's legs and purred before lifting his face to receive the fish.

"Wow, you have a cat," Ava said. "I haven't seen many animals since I arrived, and someone told me there were no cats here. I guess she was wrong, by at least one."

"Animals in Pie Town include Harvey, Lola, our lone coyote that we've never seen but who calls to us from the desert, and now Broussard."

"How did Lola get here?" Ava asked.

"Lola is different from the others. She is what we call dream-made."

"What's that mean?"

"It means she was brought into being by Jack and Annie, born of love and memories," Jasmine explained.

"That's . . . Wow. That's romantic. I don't use that word very often."

"You're right, though, it is deeply romantic," Jasmine agreed. "The rest of us can't perform that particular magic. It requires experiences of the outside world which we lack—having loved and having lost. Jack and Annie summoned Lola from the ashes of their sorrow: one version of her, anyway."

Ava couldn't speak. She swallowed hard and rubbed a hand across her face.

"Broussard is not exactly mine, and he hasn't met anyone else yet. He is my friend, and he is welcome to stay however long he likes. I told him that. He was making a ruckus at night, trying to get through the Door. I used to be scared, thinking it was a monster; probably because I've watched too many horror flicks over at Cinema Retrograde.

Eventually, I recognized the sound as being cat-like, which is also thanks to the movies.

"I decided to open the Door one evening. I was frightened that first time because I couldn't be sure that the scratching and yowling were feline. Anyway, this sweet fellow came through. After that, I asked our local handyman, Sid, to build a pet door. I'd seen one of those in the movies, too, but I had to draw it so that Sid knew what I wanted. As far as I know, it's the only pet door in Pie Town."

Ava watched Broussard cleaning his paws. "How'd you know his name? Is it on his collar?"

"Collar?" Jasmine glanced at the pale blue collar with the silver bell on it that encircled Broussard's neck. "Oh, no. He told me when we first met. It suits you well, doesn't it, you elegant puss?" Jasmine stroked the cat who was purring like an engine now. She picked him up and propped him on her right shoulder. He was huge, Ava thought, probably two feet long without the tail. He covered most of Jasmine's upper body. "Do you speak cat?" she asked Ava.

Ava thought about this before answering, "I just might. I seem to speak hare which is not something I knew before coming here. Maybe I can speak cat too?"

"Sure thing. The two are closely related: predominantly silent languages that require focused intent and concentration. You just have to make an effort; you'll see."

"Jasmine, where does he go back to, when he leaves here?"

Jasmine shrugged. Broussard rested his head on her shoulder.

"I've asked him that," Jasmine explained, "but he doesn't like to talk about it. Lately, he is here more often than not. He comes every evening and stays overnight with me."

Ava and Jasmine both stared at the Door through which Broussard had entered, but neither cared to open it.

"The thing is, when I did open it that first time to let him in, there was just nothing there. It was like he stepped in out of the cosmic void. There was a warm wind blowing in total blackness. But I could hear things: voices that sounded like people, or at least one person. Female. I think there might have been someone else farther away but can't say for sure; someone she was talking to maybe. She was yelling and making an awful racket, but I couldn't make out the words. It was like trying to understand someone using tin cans and string for a telephone—saw that in a movie too—only, in our version, the other person is light years away, instead of a few feet. You know?"

Ava smiled. She remembered the telephone game from childhood when Jeannie used to tie baked-bean cans together and play with her. Her mother: her only friend. Ava put her hand to her heart reflexively, soothing a pang of longing for Jeannie. "Sure, I know that game. You haven't opened the Door since then?"

"No. Sid, our handyman—who looks like Sol over at the drugstore, by the way—must have opened it to install the cat door, but I was working in my store at the time, and he never mentioned it. I just gave him the plans and left him to it."

The cat's door had not closed fully and, as if on cue, a lone voice began seeping through the gap: a screeching soprano. Broussard hissed and leaped out of Jasmine's arms, disappearing beneath a nearby divan. Ava reached down and pressed the door closed before latching it in place, which muffled the sound.

"Thanks, Ava." Jasmine looked at the Door again, and Ava noticed she was gnawing her bottom lip with her teeth.

"I keep telling him he doesn't have to leave. I don't know why he goes back every day, except that cats are territorial. He probably resents his home life being wrecked by that person who never seems to talk without screaming. Though, that's not entirely fair since maybe the only time we can hear her is when she's loud. I guess that's possible."

"Maybe," Ava replied, but neither of them believed this.

"Would you mind closing the ceiling too? We're expecting showers."

"Sure thing," Ava replied, though wondered how there could be showers in this town of static weather. "It's a strange sky, Jasmine."

"Yes. Way up here is an unfamiliar heaven, isn't it?" Jasmine captured Ava's gaze with her own. "You'll come to love it, I promise. Now, my friends, dinner is ready."

Jasmine crouched down and peered beneath the divan. "Broussy, we have pizza, and you know it's your favorite." The moment he heard *pizza*, the cat reappeared and shot down the spiral staircase.

"Would you look at him go? Hooray for pizza, I say."

"Always," replied Ava.

Sixteen

The three of them sat in Jasmine's lounge room on a cream leather couch, eating pizza and getting better acquainted. Ava was not surprised to learn that Jasmine had never been a child and so had never had parents. Somehow, she'd worked that out already by the time it came up.

"No family and no family name, only the name I came into the world with: Jasmine. If you want to, though, you can call me Jas, like all my close friends do."

Jasmine was not surprised to learn that Ava had felt increasingly confused about her identity, her life, and her mental stability ever since arriving in Pie Town. She was unable to shed much light, though, on the film that Ava had watched, as an audience of one, at Cinema Retrograde.

"And then Angie—You know Angie, with the electric-blue hair?" Ava asked.

"Sure," Jasmine answered, sprinkling cheese on another slice of pizza. "We all know each other."

"Okay, so Angie said, 'This is not your story, Ava,'" Ava said, feeling upset all over again hearing herself repeat it. "But I don't understand. Why was I led into a cinema to watch a hodgepodge movie that includes my birth, if it's 'not my story'?"

"Oh, I see," Jasmine answered. She set down her pizza and wiped her hands on a napkin.

"You do?" Ava set down her pizza, too, and sat up straighter to listen.

"Maybe I do. Were you asking Angie what it all meant? The movie, I mean? Were you hoping she could explain it to you?"

Ava thought back and felt inexplicably embarrassed, "Sure I was. She was the only one there."

Jasmine met Ava's eyes. "Ava, sometimes we have a message to give to our visitors, but that is all that we have. You follow?"

Ava wasn't sure that she did, so she said, "Maybe . . . No, I don't know."

"You know the saying, 'Don't shoot the messenger'? I've heard it in movies quite a few times, so I think it's common."

"Oh," Ava answered. She thought about this for a minute, sorting through the implications. She remembered Jeannie having to explain that expression to her repeatedly before she could comprehend its usage in modern contexts. It was not meant to be taken literally because nobody shot messengers these days. Probably. Ava thought about Harvey and the kind of people who hunted hares. She sighed. Idioms were hard work. "You're saying that the movie was Angie's message to deliver, like when Harvey delivers messages, but that she doesn't necessarily understand the message any better than I do?"

"That's what I am saying," Jasmine smiled.

"How do I find out who sent the message? I thought maybe Evelyn was behind it but—"

"Ava, if you got a message delivered like that, it could only be from one source," Jasmine explained.

"Who?"

"Pie Town, Ava. The town is talking to you."

"The town?" Ava gaped at Jasmine and then closed her mouth, realizing how unattractive she must look. She grabbed a napkin, in case she had tomato sauce and anchovy stuck to her face.

"Sure thing," Jasmine answered. "But this isn't the best news ever because it tends to communicate in oblique gestures and abstract symbols." Jasmine grimaced, and Ava thought she knew why.

"I'm not good at . . ." Ava trailed off. She sighed. Even the cat was staring at her.

"Subtlety, ambiguity, or abstraction," Jasmine finished for her. "Yes, I've gathered that. Okay, so we have to figure out another way, don't we?"

Ava felt her heart lift, "We do?"

"Sure thing," Jasmine replied. Ava wanted to hug her but wasn't sure it would be okay, so she stuffed the last of her pizza in her mouth instead. Broussard had no such worries. Ava watched as he leaped onto Jasmine's lap and began kneading her right thigh through her jeans.

Jasmine scratched Broussard's ears while sipping her drink, and then seemed to come to a decision.

"You want to know where the Doors open to?" she asked Ava.

Ava nodded.

"To stranger places than here, I think," Jasmine explained. "But then, I guess any place that's not home seems strange to most people, right?"

"You mean you've never crossed one of the thresholds yourself?" Ava asked.

"Holy hotcakes!" Jasmine looked horrified. "No, no one has. I won't say we never open them just enough to poke our heads in from time to time, but that's been sufficient to dissuade us. They're unstable. They can morph from one environment into something entirely different, in no time flat. Frequently, we encounter empty blue or pink or orange skies, and winds of varying force and temperature. Sometimes, we can hear sounds from distant oceans, and birds singing, or voices murmuring. But we never see the origins of the sounds and, even when we use a telescope, we can see nothing beyond the sherbet-colored skies. We've never stepped across a threshold. There are limits to our curiosity."

"Seriously? You live with all these Doors, and you've never?" Ava asked. Immediately, she regretted sounding incredulous. Would she have stepped through herself, without being sure what she'd meet on the other side? She thought about the screeching voice behind Broussard's Door. Probably not.

"There's a lot about life we can't understand or explain, Ava, but for those of us who've known no other home, it's just our normal world, you know? There are things which bring us pleasure and things we fear, just like you. Not understanding stuff is typical for us, just as it is for most people, probably. People like you, who wander in from the outer desert, seem to think you've entered a world where everyone has all the answers. It's like you want us to tell you the truth about something. We answer what questions we can, but can you imagine trying to explain your world to me, comprehensively?"

"No," Ava admitted, "there's a lot I don't understand."

"Exactly. We are part of this place we call Pie Town, and it is part of us. But we don't comprehend it entirely, and maybe we never will. The off-world visitors don't ask for explanations but tend to accept things as they are. They have more experience with the universe at large than our outer-desert friends. That's not meant to be insulting but merely factual."

"I'm not insulted," Ava answered. "But at least one person here knows things about me, personally, that I need to understand."

"That is a fact. Someone does. You belong here, Ava, or you wouldn't be here. And since you're newly arrived, you've been assigned a host. It's through your host that you'll find the thread of your story."

"I see," Ava answered. She knew that her hostess was Evelyn, who was about as good at the job as Ava would have been herself. And yet, if Evelyn could lead Ava to the thread of her story, at least it meant that Ava had a story. In liminal moments between waking and sleeping, she'd started to feel like an indistinct entity with no life of her own.

"When you seek specific answers from us, Ava, we may or may not have them. But even if we do, it is not always appropriate for us to share them. Some things are not ours to say. That is the way of our town and its people."

"I see," Ava said again. She felt overwhelmed, and too many thoughts were tumbling through her mind for her to say more. She longed to pull out her notebook and pen from her backpack, but she didn't want to display her list-writing compulsion to Jasmine.

"Having said that, if you ask about topics of general interest, you're likely to be given plenty of answers—more than you can handle, probably. Whether they make sense or have any relationship to reality is a whole other question."

Ava thought again of Evelyn.

"At our collective heart, we are a simple people, despite all the smart-sounding theories you hear around town. We pretend to be deeply philosophical to impress the tourists. Besides, writing the *Gazette* gives the three Ms something to do while eating pie, drinking coffee, and speculating on the nature of the universe.

"We townies are not worldly types. We don't travel outside our borders. None of us has ever zoomed along the superhighway, hitched a ride through the outer desert, stepped through a Door, or boarded the Infinite Loop. People come and go from here, but we remain committed homebodies and armchair adventurers."

Jasmine paused to stroke Broussard, who had fallen asleep on her lap. Then she looked at Ava with a serious expression and said, "For all that we do not know, though, there is one thing we know absolutely: you should never exit through any Door from which you did not enter. None of us, the twenty-one original townsfolk, came through Doors, so that leaves us out entirely. And none of these particular Doors are entry points for our outer-desert friends."

"How did you get here, Jasmine? All of those whom you call the 'original townsfolk,' or 'townies'?" Ava asked.

Jasmine gave a gentle shrug and continued talking, as though Ava had not spoken.

"These Doors were built to keep others out, rather than let them in, is what I am telling you. Even though we built them, we don't know much about where they lead. The town provided the plan, and the three Ms supervised the construction. We hired laborers from off-world. They brought their own materials and completed the whole job whippy-snippy. After that, things calmed down around here, and life became much more peaceful and predictable, which is just how we like it."

Ava was about to say that she was finding Pie Town anything but predictable when Jasmine slid out from under Broussard and leaped to her feet, exclaiming, "Here it is! Come, be quick!" She reached out a hand to Ava, who took it, and they bolted up the spiral staircase that was on the opposite side of the apartment from the one Ava had used before. Jasmine led them to a section of the balcony that Ava thought would have been just above the front windows of the shop, had the shop still existed. Between a seaweed-green Door that looked cobbled together out of driftwood and another that she guessed was carved onyx, there hung a curtain which Ava had not seen earlier: a sumptuous brocade of deep blue silk with gold and silver stars splashed across it.

"These curtains are beautiful," Ava remarked, running her fingers along the edge of the fabric and peering closely at a star which was just about at eye level.

"Thanks. I made them myself," Jasmine replied.

Jasmine moved ahead, pulling back one side of the drapery and stepping into the opening but then pausing to peer up at Ava and give her a look that Ava could not quite read. Concern? Fear?

"What is it?" Ava asked.

"I want to share this with you because it's a wonder to behold, but the first thing I need you to know is that you are safe with me. Okay?"

Ava nodded and smiled, then squeezed Jasmine's hand gently. "I believe you," she said and meant it.

"Will you close your eyes?" Jasmine asked.

Ava hesitated only slightly before nodding and shutting her eyes. She felt Jasmine's tug on her hand and the brush of silk against her face as they moved through the curtains.

"Now, Ava, I am going to place you in front of a big divan, and once you feel it against the back of your legs, it will be safe to sit down or fall backward, or whatever you feel like doing. Got it?"

"Yes," Ava answered. Jasmine had slipped an arm around her waist and was walking her carefully across a surface that felt cool and slightly slippery beneath Ava's feet.

Within moments, Ava felt the divan against her calves and lowered herself onto it.

"Can I open my eyes?" She asked.

"You can, but remember what I said about being safe," Jasmine answered.

Ava wondered if she were going to open her eyes to a roomful of free-range venomous snakes, or something equally horrific. She remembered that she did not know Jasmine all that well and that Pie Town was the freakiest place she'd ever been. But then she felt Jasmine settling down next to her on the divan and decided that, yes, she did trust her to keep her safe.

Taking a deep breath, Ava opened her eyes.

"Behold the universe!" Jasmine proclaimed, laughing and holding out her arms in an expansive gesture, as though offering Ava a great gift which, in her way, she was.

Ava gasped. The two of them were seated on a divan, sure enough, but they were surrounded in every direction by nothing but the vast cosmic night.

Ava felt something then that she'd never felt before: awe, in the truest sense of the word. She turned to Jasmine, her astonished face asking a hundred wordless questions.

"Ava, you are so animated when you're surprised," Jasmine said. "I'd never fully grasped what phrases like 'eyes wide as flying saucers' and 'mouth like a gaping black hole' meant until I met you."

She grasped Ava's trembling hands in her steady ones before continuing. "The reason I said to remember that you are safe with me is that, right now, you think you are free floating in outer space on a magic sky bed. That would be alarming to any sane person. But rest assured that we've not left our familiar galaxy or even our solar system and that there's a solid floor beneath us. We're enclosed by an impenetrable glass capsule. You can't see the structural elements, but they are there, nonetheless. If you put your feet flat, you will find that the floor still exists, and if you walk a few feet in any direction, or stand on your tiptoes and reach up as high as you can, you will come up against indestructible surfaces. Also, as promised, it's safe as houses. Is that how that saying goes?"

Ava nodded. She knew this expression but had never understood it, since she'd gleaned from an early age that not all houses were safe. If the *Three Little Pigs* had taught her anything, besides the regrettable truth that wolves were much maligned and badly treated, it was that some houses were no protection at all.

Jasmine continued chattering away as Ava glanced around her, trying to convince herself to stand. Wrought iron lanterns hung above them, suspended from nothing, as far as Ava could tell. Their still light illuminated the red, cream, and gold divan, with its tasseled pillows, which reminded Ava of Marrakech. The blue curtains, which should have been visible just a few feet behind the divan, had disappeared.

"The town made the capsule, of course, not me. In fact, the town made the whole structure that we call my apartment, including the Doors, as I've already explained. I am the privileged caretaker of all this grandeur, but my creative talents extend not much farther than pizza and draperies. The original building that houses my grocery store and the rooms above it was not made by the town, though. It has been here always, from the beginning of everything."

Ava was only half listening, unable to focus on Jasmine's words. She regretted having left her three Marys back at the camper, in her travel pack, because they would have brought comfort, as she hovered in space with her new friend. Ava pictured the Marys' solemn faces and focused on her breathing. She counted to twelve, silently, while pressing her feet to the floor and willing herself to stand.

Once vertical, Ava stretched to touch the ceiling and felt her tension easing as she reached it. Things were just as Jasmine had described, so far. Intuitively, Ava knew that the physical reassurance of walls and floors would help her cope with the existential enormity of this experience. She began to slide her feet softly across the floor until she reached the curved wall of the capsule. There, she stopped and began turning slowly in a circle, gazing around her at the infinite wonder of space.

"Ava, are you okay? You look . . . Terrified is the word that comes to mind."

Ava nodded. "I'm just . . . I've never . . . I don't . . . I can't . . . Yes, I'm fine." Now, as always, concise answers were best.

"Please, come over here with me and watch because what's happening now really is magical," Jasmine replied.

Ava tiptoed delicately back to Jasmine's side, as though walking too heavily might crack open a chasm in the glass capsule and send them flailing into the freezing, naked night of space. Just as she reached the divan, Jasmine leaped up saying, "I almost forgot."

Ava was reassured to glimpse the drapes flickering in and out of view as Jasmine's left arm drew back a swathe of fabric, and her right hand slipped through the gap to retrieve a large wooden bowl filled with popcorn. That meant that Jasmine's apartment was still there, even if it was currently out of sight.

Despite her nervousness, Ava laughed. "You have such a sense of occasion, Jasmine."

Jasmine settled onto the divan and patted the space next to her. "Just lie back and look up, my friend. Nothing is better than this, I promise."

Ava crawled onto the divan and lay back on the pillows, next to Jasmine.

"You see? You see?" Jasmine asked, brimming with excitement and pointing overhead. "It's revving up now. The few I spotted from downstairs were just the beginning."

Ava did see and was once again overcome. The sky was alive with the most spectacular meteor shower she had ever witnessed. Soaring fast and bright across their field of vision were hundreds of shining meteors; so many that the night seemed lit up loud, while conversation inside the capsule dropped to a church whisper.

"The Perseids?" Ava asked, as quietly as she could manage.

"Sure thing," Jasmine replied, and passed Ava the popcorn.

Seventeen

As Ava stepped out onto the landing to start the long descent to the ground floor, Jasmine answered a question that she'd nearly forgotten she'd asked, "We've been here for as far back as we can remember, Ava, the original twenty-one. We emerged with the town, and it's the only home we've ever known. Just please don't ask me when that was, okay?" Jasmine stretched up on her toes to kiss Ava's cheek, which was some effort since Ava had put her heels back on.

Before Ava could respond, Jasmine slipped back into her apartment and closed the door. Ava stood facing the bright red door, her eyes locked on the brass knocker. Impulsively, she reached for it, intending to bang it against the door, to beseech Jasmine to open it again so that she might offer a more gracious "thank you and goodnight" than the silence she'd exchanged for the kiss.

But instead, faster than her brain could figure out what it was doing, Ava's hand dropped from the knocker to the stenciled black branch beneath it. *Where's the blackbird gone?* She peered at the branch, brushing her index finger back and forth across it, and then lifted the knocker to peek beneath it. The finely stenciled creature who'd been perched on the branch to greet her when she'd reached Jasmine's door had disappeared as completely and inexplicably as a magician's assistant from a magic box.

Ava glanced to her left and discovered her friend perched on the wall near the stair handrail, looking poised for flight. She was sure she recognized him from the door, even though he looked strikingly like the other members of his flock. Ava paused, remembering what Jasmine had told her about how people from off-world just accepted things as they happened in Pie Town. Feeling that it would be easy to crush the life from this delicate mystery, she decided to follow the example of those strangers from off. She nodded to the blackbird as she might to any fellow traveler and then began her descent, accompanied by fluttering shadows in her peripheral vision and an occasional echoing twitter. Whenever she stopped moving for a while, which she found necessary due to the incredible length of the journey, the bird would rest with her, becoming once again a matte silhouette on an unremarkable gray wall. This gentle trickery felt less reminiscent of Alfred Hitchcock than Charlie Chaplin, and Ava was glad to have the company.

Reaching the ground floor after what seemed like hours, Ava threw open the heavy door, eager for fresh night air. A shadowy flutter near her face let her know that her friend had emerged, too, free from his post in the stairwell and thrillingly skyborne. Ava's heart sank as she registered her second failed parting of the night, having offered no goodbye or thank you to her companion.

Her thoughts flitted back to her evening with Jasmine, as she strolled through the garden behind the grocery, running her hand over the basil and waking up its scent. She was lost in thought by the time she reached the camper, so the sound of motion nearby startled her. Harvey hopped forward with an apologetic look.

"Hello, Harvey," Ava said. "You did spook me a little, but there's no need to apologize. I was thinking and not paying attention to—Hey! Did I just understand you?"

Harvey blinked.

"I've been practicing speaking cat this evening, you know. Well, no, you probably wouldn't know, unless you speak cat too." Ava paused and began again with, "Hi, Harvey."

She felt sure that he returned her greeting and sent a thought to her, silently: *I have a message for you.*

"Do you want to come in?"

They settled on the camper's red couch, and Ava lifted the flap of Harvey's carrier pouch to extract a tangerine-coloured envelope with the three-hares crest on the back. She understood that Harvey wanted her to read the message and send a reply. *I'm either adept at hare-speak or inventing conversations.* She could swear that she heard Harvey's thought-voice giggle.

The message was an invitation from Evelyn for lunch the following day.

"Should I write a reply?" she asked.

I can let her know if you just tell me, the thought-voice said.

"Okay. Please tell Evelyn I'll be there. I wanted to talk to her anyway."

Harvey hopped back onto his feet and inclined his head to her.

"Are you off already?" she asked.

It is late.

"Would you like some carrots? For the road?"

Harvey gave her his bright-eyed look, his nose twitching. She tucked a few carrot sticks into his carrier pouch and asked silently: *Can you hear my thoughts, Harvey?*

Only when you want me to, replied Harvey, and then he was hopping away.

"Well, now that's something," Ava said aloud.

She woke up the next morning on the lounger beside the pool. She'd been restless after Harvey left and had wandered over to the recreation area, carrying her orange notebook in one hand and a lantern she'd found in the camper in the other. She'd had two things in mind: one, to write a list; two, to see if the pool at the RV park had the same effect on her as the pool at the motel. She hadn't planned to swim. If this pool did have the same mesmerizing quality as the infinity pool, swimming in it alone could be dangerous. She'd sat at the edge of the pool's deep end with her legs dangling in the water, staring at the light shining up from the bottom. She couldn't have said how long she waited to feel or see something, anything, which might remind her of the infinity pool, but it was long enough that she began to nod off with boredom. Eventually, she'd settled into a lounger and, by the light of the lantern glow, written a list of things she liked about Jasmine. After that, she had fallen asleep watching the lights in the sky.

Ava took a quick shower and pulled on her goldfinch t-shirt, last night's jeans, and a pair of robin's-egg-blue sneakers. After dressing, she walked over to the diner and settled into her booth, where she sipped coffee and reviewed her plans for the day: play with Lola, lunch with Evelyn, and meet Jasmine at dusk. She tapped her pen rhythmically on the page and read it again, unable to shake off the nagging feeling that she was forgetting something. She tried to focus on enjoying her breakfast, perfect in its simplicity, but as she peeled her boiled egg, the feeling persisted. She shook her head like a wet dog, trying to clear it, and glanced around to see if anyone had noticed.

The only other customers were the three Ms in their bowler hats. As usual, they were sitting at the counter, leaning ever so slightly toward each other, but not speaking. Although they never so much as glanced her way, Ava suspected that they were acutely aware of her and everything else that went on.

Julie was in the kitchen. She'd rushed off with an apologetic smile, muttering something about a big to-go order. Ava wondered just how far away it was going. She finished her breakfast and slid out of the booth, feeling the attention of the Ms follow her out the door.

Lola was waiting at the door of Cafe Z when Ava arrived, and she was unabashedly happy to see her. They walked over to Skylights Park where, as their first activity, Ava decided to try her new communication skills with the setter. Ava settled on the grass with her legs crossed. Lola sat back on her hind legs, facing Ava. Ava began by staring intensely into Lola's big brown eyes. Lola panted and stared back, her mouth hanging open and her tongue lolling out the right side.

Ava tried sending the thought *Lola, can you hear me?* Lola stared back at Ava for several silent heartbeats, her doggy eyes brimming with trust and love. Her expression reminded Ava of how Lola looked when she hadn't yet grasped a new game they were playing.

Ava tried again. *Is there anything you'd like to tell me?* Nothing.

Maybe I should try barking and woofing? Still nothing.

Hey, Lola, want a treat? When that didn't work, Ava knew her approach was a flop. Maybe dogs didn't need to communicate with humans the same way cats and hares did. After all, it was always easy to tell what Lola wanted or needed, without telepathy.

Ava held open her arms and said, "Come here, you sweet, beautiful girl."

Lola sprang forward, knocking Ava backward, and began licking her face vigorously until Ava surrendered.

They tussled on the ground, played fetch until they were both panting, and then walked to the RV park, where Lola retrieved a water toy from the pool repeatedly until flopping down exhausted at Ava's feet. Ava took the hint and collapsed into a lounge chair where, with the dog asleep beside her, she dozed off.

Ava dropped off Lola at Cafe Z on her way to the No Vacancy Motel. She'd thought about taking Lola to lunch with her but then decided against it. Evelyn and dogs didn't strike her as a natural fit, and she didn't want to upset Harvey. Nevertheless, it was one of Ava's personal goals to bring Lola and Harvey together. She knew they could be friends if Lola refrained from leaping on Harvey and licking him too much.

Ava was pleased to be adjusting to the town's rhythms. She managed to arrive poolside just as Evelyn walked up with a platter of sandwiches, fruit, and iced drinks. Evelyn set down the lunch tray to give Ava a quick hug and an air kiss near each cheek. Then, holding Ava at arm's length, she said, "Well, my stars, Ava! Don't you look good! Pie Town has that effect on everyone, of course."

"Does it? I was going to ask you about that because I've been feeling better and better ever since I arrived. Today, I feel fantastic," Ava replied. Then, knowing it was polite to repay a compliment with a compliment, Ava said, "You look good, too, Evelyn."

Evelyn did look good. She was wearing an orange bikini with a big, floppy hat, white sunglasses, and a white linen shirt. Her nails were painted pale blue, to match her lips. Not for the first time, Ava wondered if Evelyn's Southern accent was genuine. Like lipstick, it was sometimes thickly applied and other times soft and light. Ava was still amazed that someone who looked so much like her could look so unlike her. She thought that Evelyn looked like the kind of girl she might have been, too, if she were a "real" California girl.

"You are more of a real girl now than you've ever been, Ava Louise, with or without California," Evelyn answered, as if Ava had spoken aloud.

Ava grimaced but said nothing. This one-way telepathy was unlike her silent conversations with Harvey. Harvey did not intrude into her thoughts, but Evelyn barged right on in.

"Now, Ava, don't get mad at me. I almost can't help it. It's our connection, and there's nothing we can do about it, either of us. Come and sit down, please. Let's have lunch and visit. You wanted to talk to me, and it's time." Evelyn stopped and looked at her quizzically, touching one finger to Ava's cheek. "Have you forgotten something else? Or lost time? It wasn't my doing this time, I swear."

Ava opened and closed her mouth once or twice before saying "Yes. I've felt all day like I've forgotten something or that I'm missing something important."

In an uncharacteristic move, Ava turned to face Evelyn squarely and reached out for her hands, clasping them in her own. She'd decided that if Evelyn could read her mind, maybe she could read Evelyn's mind too. What did she have to lose by trying?

The effect was immediate and shocking. Ava felt as if she had opened all the Doors in Jasmine's apartment at once. The internal current that she'd felt since arriving in Pie Town surged through her like a torrent, but she held on tight and let it come.

A series of images began to flash through her mind. She could see herself—or was it Evelyn?—inside Pie Town's chapel. The girl appeared to be sleepwalking, and one of the three Ms was helping her step up onto a dais. Ava had been in enough churches during her travels to know what altars looked like, and that they ordinarily had a cross or crucifix above them. This altar looked like a round, smooth stone, simple and bare, with no altar cloth covering it. What was truly bizarre, though, was the big, egg-shaped orb floating above it. Odd as this was, she didn't get the impression that the girl, who either was or was not herself, had been forced into this ritual. She looked tranquil as M helped her to lie down on the altar.

M stepped back, and the orb descended toward the girl. It stopped about a foot above her body before changing the direction of its movement so that it traveled up and down the length of her, streaming soft lights. The look on M's face was solemn, which made Ava think that she was witnessing a religious ceremony, even though the sacred props looked like an unholy cross between a Xerox machine and a disco ball.

Her view widened to include the sanctuary, and Ava saw that the pews were full of people. She could see their lips moving but heard nothing, as if a silent film played before her eyes. She was held spellbound until the moment the orb stopped scanning, which was when the parishioners' lips stopped moving. M reached out for the hand of the girl on the altar, shattering Ava's peace. She was overcome with dread and revulsion. Whatever was going to happen next, she knew she could not bear to see it.

Ava tried to snatch her hands away, but Evelyn grabbed her wrists. With surprising strength, Evelyn pulled Ava close enough to whisper in her ear: "You have to do this now. It's time," before shoving her backward into the waiting infinity pool.

Eighteen

She's on the beach the day after graduation, lost in thought and tired of the angst. She needs to clear her mind and escape from the relentless *what next, what next, what next* that's hounded her throughout this last month of high school.

She paddles out three hundred feet or so and manages to catch a big wave just before it breaks. She pops onto her feet and steadies herself on her new board, a graduation gift from her mom. For a few exhilarating seconds, she's flying high, enjoying her freedom, the wind whipping her hair, and the broad expanse of empty sea. Only then does she wonder why it's empty; not only the ocean but the beach, too, as far as she can see in every direction.

This moment of distraction costs her dearly. Before she can master her wave, it folds in on her and sends her tumbling like a sock in a washing machine. The board thumps hard against her left temple, and she grasps her head, forgetting to swim. She sinks beneath the roiling foam of breaking waves, and everything goes dark.

Where's the sun? Which way to air?

She wonders fleetingly if she will die here, in this familiar stretch of ocean only a few miles from home, where she's come off her board dozens of times in the past, but never like this. The blackness and disorientation are total. It feels like the sea wants to keep her. She struggles to surface but, as though colluding with the turbulent water, her board returns to thwack her again, this time on her right temple. She reaches out in confusion, trying to get a grip on the board, but it's gone. With strength born of panic, she breaststrokes upward, only to find herself colliding with sand instead of sky. As she spins around in the slow motion of all movement underwater, she knows that she won't make it to the surface alive. Her lungs feel fit to burst, and she still can't see. She struggles to stabilize her feet on the sandy ocean floor, her last thought being to launch herself toward light and air; instead, she blacks out. Her body begins to sink, her mouth dropping open to the sea.

She opens her eyes to a glowing sphere floating in the dark water about a foot above her head. It's creamy white and faintly glowing, like a celestial egg. She finds its soft light soothing, and she is no longer afraid. She is lying flat on her back, and when she moves her hands, she feels stone beneath her. The orb begins to hum. It moves up and down the length of her body but never touches her.

Ava wonders what will happen to them now, Lolo and herself. Being the most deeply buried aspect of Lolo's consciousness, Ava's role is largely that of the silent observer. Still, she has her own ideas and preferences, and she tries to influence the course of their shared existence by gentle persuasion. She thinks of Lolo as a sister, the dynamic sibling who shows her face to the world while Ava remains hidden. There is a third sibling, Evelyn, who lives closer to the surface of Lolo's mind, but she is unknown to Ava.

Lolo, unlike most other human beings, has been fully aware of all three aspects of her consciousness from the day she was born, sensing their presence before she even had words to explain them to herself. Her mother, Jeannie, loved to tell the story of how her labor was triggered by an earthquake that hit Catalina Island while she was on a day trip with a friend whose identity she never revealed. There was a medical clinic on the island, and the birth had been surprisingly fast for a first child, but the continuing tremors and the shock of her baby's early arrival had frazzled Jeannie. She'd struggled to decide quickly between the three names she had chosen: Louise, Evelyn, and Ava. She said each of them aloud while looking at her daughter, trying to determine which name suited her and whether the baby seemed to have a preference.

"Are you Louise? Evelyn? Ava?" As Jeannie whispered to her baby, the child opened her eyes and looked at her calmly. Jeannie could have sworn she smiled at all three names, but she knew the nurse would say it was gas.

"She likes all of them. We'll take them all," Jeannie concluded, as if deciding on shoes at a clearance sale. *But in what order?* Jeannie asked herself. "I need time to think," she said to the young nurse, just as another aftershock shook the small building.

"We need to get this done and get you out of here," replied the nurse. The nurse was distressed by the quake, too, and rushing through the birth certificate. She had nodded a few times to indicate she was listening but had not looked up from her computer as she typed. She asked Jeannie whether she had picked a middle name. "Yes, okay. . . Yes . . . I think I like 'Louise' best as her middle name, after my mother and me. My mother's name was 'Yvette Louise,' and mine is 'Jean Louise,'" Jeannie had answered.

The nurse nodded again but kept typing. Moments later, she was printing out the certificate and handing it to Jeannie to review, which Jeannie did with a cursory glance. After the attending physician and nurse superintendent had signed the certificate, it was made official with the hospital seal and secured in a brown envelope. "Here's your copy, Ms. Pembroke," the nurse said. "I'll send one to the state registrar for filing. The air ambulance is on its way, and we'll have you and your baby out of here as soon as possible, to a safer location."

Two days later, from the comfort of her home, Jeannie had remembered the certificate and pulled it out of the backpack she'd been carrying on the island. She'd taken to calling her baby "Louise" as soon as she'd brought her home. It just seemed to fit. But she had to laugh when she read the birth certificate, which recorded her daughter's name as "Louise Louise" with an asterisk beside it. At the bottom of the certificate was an added line of text, with an asterisk, which read "Others: Ava Louise, Evelyn Louise."

When the state registrar called Jeannie for clarification, they insisted she decide on a single first and middle name. Jeannie had chosen "Louise Louise," liking the musicality of it. From the day she started speaking, though, Louise Louise referred to herself as "Lolo," and that's the name that stuck. Jeannie would always feel sentimental about the original hospital certificate, the one with the three names on it that she kept in her box of treasures. As for Lolo, she would always insist that this certificate was, in fact, the correct version.

Ava remembers that birth certificate as she lies flat on her back on the stone slab beneath the waves and listens to the orb humming above her. She doesn't notice when it stops moving because she is wondering, for the first time, about that third name on Lolo's birth certificate: *"Evelyn Louise."* An existential chasm opens in Ava as she wonders why, since she is real, Evelyn would not be real too. *But then, if she exists as part of Lolo, why wouldn't I know? And why can't I feel Lolo now? Is she sleeping?* A brief surge of panic threatens to swallow Ava whole, but it's obliterated by an abrupt physical wrenching that feels like dying.

With no understanding of what's happening, Ava feels herself rising like a ghost from the stone, alone: an Ava independently embodied, which she has never been. She steps warily onto the ocean floor. She doesn't ask herself why she can breathe and walk perfectly upright against the push and pull of the water because she believes that she and Lolo must be dead or dreaming. If this is a dream, it can only be a nightmare. *Where is Lolo?* Ava turns to look at the stone from which she has just risen, but it's no longer there. As she glances up at the orb, it disappears too. Blackness engulfs her again.

An image flickers in the darkness, in her mind or the ocean; she's not sure which because she can no longer tell whether her eyes are open. She expects a jellyfish or an eel, but it is not a marine creature floating in her vision. She is surprised to recognize that it's a hand-drawn map, but she can see it clearly and even understands its symbols. There's a red line marking out a route that leads directly from their home to someplace they've never been. She wonders if that is where Lolo has disappeared to, in this terrible dream. The destination has no label, just the glowing enchantment of the bright red line, but nothing has ever felt so much like a personal invitation. She reaches for the map.

Ava opens her eyes on the beach, rolls over, and vomits saltwater until she's empty. Her surfboard rests nearby, still attached to her ankle by its leash. Her dive watch has stopped, so she has no idea how long she's been lying here, but she can see the sun beginning to set. She can't remember how she got back to the beach. She remembers coming off her board, she remembers the frothing chaos that followed, and she remembers the moment she realized she was drowning, but there's nothing after that.

That evening she will tell her mother that she is going traveling throughout the South and Southwest. She will leave Jeannie waving at the bus station, shouting "Postcards, Ava, remember the postcards!" one last time before she's out of sight.

Nineteen

Something was slapping her in the face, and she could hear screaming nearby. Ava opened her eyes to Jack's dreadlocks whipping across her cheeks as he carried her out of the pool.

"She's okay!" Jack announced, and Ava looked around to where he was looking, over by the loungers where she'd been standing with Evelyn, right before Evelyn pushed her into the pool. Evelyn was still there but so was Jasmine, who was glowering at her.

Jack walked the last several feet to where the women were standing and deposited Ava onto a lounger. Ava rubbed her eyes and took a long hard look at Evelyn, "Why'd you do that? Why'd you shove me in?"

"Holy hotcakes!" Jasmine shouted. "Not only were you just sitting here by the side of the pool, calmly watching her drown, but you shoved her in?" Evelyn flinched. "What is the matter with you?"

Evelyn stepped away from Jasmine, yelling, "I had to! Let me explain!"

"She could have died in there!"

"No, Jasmine, no," Evelyn replied, softly this time. "That's not true. She would not have died. Even if Jack and you had not come running, Ava would have been fine. I promise."

Jasmine arched her brow and scowled at Evelyn, but Jack cut her off before she could say anything else.

"Evelyn is right," he said calmly.

"You're taking her side? Jack, if Harvey hadn't come for me, and I hadn't grabbed you on the way—"

"Ava would have been fine, as Evelyn said, but probably pretty soggy," Jack answered. "We should have known the pool would keep her safe. It's the beating heart of the town, after all, and the town wants her here; that's obvious. I know she looked dead from up here, but when I got to her, she was breathing. It was like a bubble of air had enclosed her head. Her eyes were open, but nobody was home. Even when I got hold of her, she didn't respond, not until we got far enough up the steps to be clear of the water."

Jasmine collapsed next to Ava, on the foot of the lounger. "Ava, I'm so glad you're okay. I was scared."

Ava smiled at her and took her hand. "Thanks, Boop. I would have missed you, too, if I'd died," she said.

"Wow, that was almost like a joke," Evelyn added. She perched on the edge of the lounger across from them. Jack gestured to her to move over and joined her there. Harvey watched silently from the spot near the table between them, nibbling grapes from the lunch that hadn't been eaten.

"I never knew you," Ava said quietly, staring at Evelyn.

"No, you didn't," Evelyn replied, just as quietly. "That was nobody's fault; it's just how things were for us. But I knew you, always. I could feel you there, silently watching the world go by, nurturing your hopes and dreams and suffering your own losses. We both loved you, Ava, even though you were only aware of one of us."

"What's happened to Lolo?" Ava asked then, realizing how frightened she was to hear the answer.

"Nothing! Or, rather, a lot. But only good things. She's been traveling the universe, that's all." Evelyn reached for the pitcher of lemonade she'd made for lunch and poured Ava a glassful.

"Oh." Ava wasn't sure how she felt about that. She drank her lemonade and thought she might cry.

"Should we leave you two alone to talk?" Jack asked, ignoring Jasmine's glare.

"No, you don't have to go. I appreciate you saving me, Jack, even if I wasn't dying. Thanks for that," Ava answered and then looked at Jasmine. "Thanks to you too."

"I didn't do anything," Jasmine answered, "but you're welcome all the same."

"You looked ready to punch Evelyn on my behalf, and that's pretty sweet of you," Ava said. They all laughed, except Evelyn.

Evelyn sat up straight and addressed Ava directly, ignoring the other two. "You had to know about us, Ava, and I promised you that you would know if you were patient and if you trusted me enough to let things unfold over time. I did say that I would show you, didn't I?"

"That's true," Ava answered. "To be fair, that is precisely what you said. Now I understand more about us and more about myself than I ever have. But I still don't understand how you two ended up here in Pie Town, while I was left behind in California with our life, our memories, and our mother. How could Mom have been calling me Ava, anyway? She never knew us as Ava."

"Yes, I know. It's part of the magic," Evelyn answered.

"Magic? Is that what this is?" Ava wondered aloud.

Jasmine stood up and leaned over Ava to pull the lunch tray off the table so that she and Jack could nibble while they listened.

Evelyn grabbed a sandwich triangle before replying. "I can't think of a better word for it, can you? You weren't drowning in the infinity pool, Ava, but Lolo truly was drowning—all of us were—in the Pacific, on the day after graduation. Somehow, Pie Town reached out to us and saved our lives, but it also separated us forever. One of us had to stay behind in California."

"Why me?"

"Lolo figured that, of the three of us, you'd had the fewest opportunities to express yourself, to connect with others, and to be alive in the world. It was an act of love on her part, not careless abandon. But then, almost immediately, you set off on a journey to find her. It took you a while to make your way to Pie Town, but you made it, nonetheless.

"Of course, you didn't know she was what you were seeking because part of what happens to those left behind is that they don't remember the process. Mom, too, would not remember that you had ever been anyone other than Ava. As for our birth certificate? Your name would come first now, if anyone cared to look, with 'Louise Louise' and 'Evelyn Louise' listed as 'Others.' Even your closest friends would never know the difference."

"My closest friends? That would be our mother. You know we never had many friends," Ava replied.

Jasmine, swallowing a mouthful of bread and cheese, said, "Well, you do now."

"Hear, hear!" Jack added, passing a carrot stick to Harvey.

"Ava, you're free now," Evelyn said. "You can be yourself and nobody else. One of the reasons that's great is because, personally, I like men. And, as I think you would recall, Lolo can go either way when it comes to choosing her friends and lovers."

Ava nodded. "I know. That's how BJ happened."

"Ugh," Jasmine interjected, having heard about BJ over dinner with Ava. "She didn't deserve you."

Evelyn laughed and nodded. "You're right about that, Jasmine, even if you do sound a little bit jealous." Evelyn winked at her, and Jasmine blushed.

Ava was silent, thinking things over. Jasmine wrapped an arm through Ava's and leaned against her, while Jack and Harvey continued to snack and watch the women.

Evelyn stared hard at Ava, and Ava could tell she was rifling through her private thoughts again. Ava tried to shut her out, but she didn't know how.

"My stars, Ava," Evelyn began, "you've been all this time on your own—two years in California time, I think you said?"

Ava nodded.

"I don't clearly remember how long two years is, but it's rather a long time, isn't it?"

Ava nodded again.

"You've had two years of wandering the country, meeting new people, and making friends." Evelyn glanced pointedly at Jasmine before continuing. "And yet, still, you regret our separation?"

Ava pulled her arm away from Jasmine and stood up. She stretched and walked over to the edge of the pool, contemplating its silent depths. After a while, she cleared her throat and glanced up, noticing that the sun was beginning to set. She'd arrived here at lunchtime. She examined her skin, but there were no signs of a prolonged immersion.

Ava turned to her friends.

"This is all new to me," Ava explained. "Until now, I'd felt something missing inside me, but I never understood what it was. And then, when the infinity pool showed me that it was never a *thing* at all, but a whole other person I'd lost—Lolo—it gutted me if you want to know the truth. I relived that afternoon in the ocean when we were torn apart. We'd never been without her, Evelyn, our whole lives. Yet, by the time I woke up on the beach, I couldn't have told you she ever existed."

"You miss her still?" Jasmine asked, in a voice that was far more subdued than usual.

"Sure she does," Evelyn replied for them both. "Good heavens, girl, we'll always miss her."

"She's not come back here?" Ava asked. She felt tears welling up in her eyes and could see that Evelyn was in the same state.

Jack spoke up. "Now wait a minute. Please hold your tears, girls, or I might start crying myself."

Jasmine laughed, but her own eyes were watery too.

"I happen to know that Louise Louise is on her way here, even as we speak."

"Are you serious, Jack? There's been news?" Evelyn asked. "I have felt like she's nearby, at least in our solar system, but the last I heard from her was a few weeks ago, in a dream. We lost touch before I could find out where she was headed."

Ava thought back to her dream a night or two ago when a familiar voice had said: *"Remember we're in the dreamscape . . ."* She snapped to attention then.

"Lolo can talk to us through dreams?" Ava asked, her astonished eyes pinned on Evelyn.

"Ava darlin', she surely can," Evelyn answered. "If she's within a reasonable distance, meaning in our solar system. You and me, see, we need to be a bit closer to each other than Lolo needs to be to either of us to communicate. I can only read your thoughts and share mine with you over a few miles, at most. I think you'll be glad to know that."

Ava ignored that last comment, but she was indeed glad to hear it. "Why'd Lolo never communicate with me before, when I was out on my own in the world?

"How do you know she didn't? You might have just shrugged her off as a weird dream," Evelyn answered.

"Right," Ava answered, realizing that's exactly how she'd responded to the dream in the camper.

Jack stood up and stretched. "Annie was over at the tower in the visitor center bringing the crew breakfast when Lolo's call came through the communications system. Louise will be here for the birthday party. She said she wouldn't miss it for the universe, or something like that. You'll be happy to hear that she also mentioned presents."

"Lolo has been enjoying an indefinite holiday, too, like Rachel and Lenie," Ava mused. Evelyn and Jasmine bowed their heads and touched their hands to their hearts. Ava noticed once again that Jack did not.

"Why do you two keep doing that? What's up with the genuflecting?" she asked.

"We're not genuflecting, just paying homage," Jasmine explained.

"I don't mean any disrespect, but why? And why doesn't Jack do it?" Ava asked, realizing with surprise that she'd not felt compelled to make a list or consult her three Marys all day.

"That's easy to explain," Evelyn began, interrupting Jasmine who'd been on the verge of answering. "Remember, Ava, how I showed you the hand-drawn maps the first time you came here to the motel and explained how time here is a kind of paradox? Of course, then I made you forget our talk because I realized you were freaking out."

"How'd you do that, anyway?" Ava asked.

"It's a cheap parlor trick Lolo taught me. It's useful sometimes but, as you found out, the effects are only temporary. Anyhoo, you remember how I explained to you that Rachel and Lenie had been born here, even though they wouldn't bring the town to life until they were our age?"

Ava nodded, and images flickered through her mind of the two young women in the movie she'd seen, bent over a notebook in a cafe, laughing and talking.

"If it weren't for Rachel and Lenie, none of us would be here. They found a way, unintentionally, to access the dreamscape. They drew our town into existence, making it into a real place with real people." Evelyn glanced at Jasmine and added, "So to speak."

Jasmine scowled at her. "We are just as real as you, Evelyn Louise! You irk me sometimes. I keep telling you that we townies were here first. You'd hope we'd get some respect for that, which we do from most people, present company excepted. Even the three Ms feel that you look down on them, and they're our town fathers. It's disgraceful."

"They said that?" Evelyn replied, her brows arching in disbelief.

"Of course not," Jasmine spat back at her. "When have you ever heard them say anything? They didn't have to say it. We all know you think we are nothing more than cartoons."

"Well—" Evelyn began, but Jasmine cut her off.

"I know, Evelyn," Jasmine interrupted. "We were born of map pencils and cheap notebook paper. Our hues are not quite the same as human flesh, and we don't have parents or surnames, blah blah blah. But does an artistic birth, rather than a biological one, makes us lesser people? I think not. Besides, we have come a long way since we first emerged with the town, and we are every bit as substantial and real as

160

you are. If you don't believe me, why don't we let Ava slap you for knocking her into the pool, and then I will slap you just because I've always wanted to, and you can tell us if you feel any difference?"

"All right, all right. Calm down. I'm sorry already. My stars, you people are sensitive."

Ava grabbed Jasmine's hand and held it while Evelyn continued.

"Anyhoo, there is a kind of magic here, to be sure: something to do with how the principles of the universe operate at this particular location; also, we believe, related to the ship that crashed who knows when and made that crater where our pool is now. There's a reason it's called the infinity pool, you know. We don't swim deeper than twelve or fifteen feet. We're not exactly sure what would happen if we did, but the pool keeps us safe, and no one has ever disappeared through the hole.

"Lenie and Rachel, whom you will meet when they stop in again, mean the world to us because they have made this world possible for us. We don't worship them, but we do love them, and our ritual is our way of honoring that love while they are away from us."

"But not Jack's way?" Ava asked.

Jack was concentrating on the ground, where he was playing pick-up sticks with Harvey, using leftover carrots and celery. He glanced up at Ava. "I love them, too, but I'm not one for symbolic gestures. Besides, the four of us go back a long way, and I think Rachel and Lenie would feel weird if they saw Annie and me observing a ritual in their honor, however well meant."

Ava studied him a moment before saying, "Someday, maybe you'll tell me how you came to be here too. Assuming, of course, that it's your story to tell."

Jack laughed. "It is mine to tell, and maybe someday I'll do that. For now, though, I've got a cafe to open for dinner and a menu to plan for this birthday bash we're catering. Now, if we are all done with drowning, I'll take off."

"I need to go, too," Jasmine said, rising to her feet and giving Ava a peck on the cheek. "I left my shop open, and I need to get ready for my date tonight with a sweet girl called Ava. See you later?

Ava smiled. "Sure thing."

"Where's Harvey?" Ava asked after they'd left. "He was just here."

"He's probably sneaked into my courtyard to commune with the cat vines again. He's found a way to talk to them, can you believe it? He claims they're on good terms now, which I take to mean they won't try to devour him. But the vines are nocturnal, so he must wait until sunset to visit. They refuse to stir before dusk. I keep telling him not to turn his back on them, but he won't listen. Silly rabbit."

"Hare."

"Whatever."

"Hey, Evelyn?"

"Yes?"

"I know you said people never grow old here, or that they don't appear to, but do people ever die?"

"Yes, unfortunately. More commonly, people fail to return from a holiday, and we lose contact with them. That's why we call holidays 'indefinite,' Ava. It's our way of saying that we are expecting them back and hoping for the best. Now and then, somebody here dies by accident, and we don't know where they end up after that. It seems that, if you die here in Pie Town, you disappear, body and all. And yet, we know that some people only *arrive* here after they've died in the outer desert— or, as you and I think of it, the outside world. That's what happened to Annie."

"Jack's Annie?"

"The one and only. Anyway, you should ask Annie about it sometime. She should be the one to tell you."

"I know, I know. It's her story to tell."

"See? You're catching on to how life works here." Evelyn beamed at her, and Ava laughed.

"Okay, what's my story then? Ever since I arrived here, I've heard 'this is not your story, Ava' from just about everybody, including an origami bird and a blue-haired girl at the cinema, who tried to soften the message with free candy. Now, I realize that they were right. All our stories, until very recently, were Lolo's, not mine. And not yours, either."

"Yes, but ever since we struck out on our own, we've been writing our stories. And now this, Ava, this life right here is your story. Pie Town is your home. It's where you belong. Pie Town and Jasmine and Harvey and me, if you give us a chance. We can be your story."

"But what about Mom?" Suddenly, Ava recalled the forgotten conversation she'd had with Jeannie, using Burke's otherwise dead mobile phone. She'd been standing on the edge of town when she'd tried turning it on, anticipating failure, but the phone had lit up with her home number on display. Surprised, Ava had pressed the call button to see if she could get through, and Jeannie had answered on the first ring. Jeannie had sounded relieved to hear from her and wondered when she'd be home. Ava had promised she'd be there soon, but she'd been unable to tell her mother where she was because, when she mentioned Pie Town, the call dropped out.

"Lolo will go back to Mom and California. She'll be our face in the world again. That's what she wants, and I think it's what we want, too, right? She's had her big adventure. The last time I connected with her, she knew you were heading our way, and she was ready to go home."

"That sounds . . ." Ava paused to listen to a coyote howling.

"Sounds what?" Evelyn prompted.

"Perfect." It dawned on Ava then that, ever since Jack and Jasmine had left, the two of them had been talking without moving their lips.

Twenty

It looked as though the whole town had turned up for the birthday party, overwhelming Ava, who tended to avoid grand social events whenever possible. Jasmine's apartment was easily big enough to accommodate everyone, but the crowd of two hundred people still came as a shock. Ava stood stock-still in the doorway, resplendent in the cerulean blue sheath dress that Jasmine had whipped up for her. She was clutching Harvey's paw in one hand and Lola's leash in the other and seemed unable to move beyond the threshold. Partly, that was due to exhaustion, as she'd had to restrain Lola from chasing the fluttery stenciled blackbirds up the never-ending stairs, but anxiety also played a part.

Harvey was dashing in a jaunty red scarf and a matching fedora, worn at a rakish angle, with holes cut out for his ears. Lola was naked but for her fur, her leash, and a fresh daisy that Ava had tucked into her collar. Ava wished she felt as relaxed as her companions.

Jasmine was at Ava's side in a heartbeat, hugging her and whispering, "Happy Birthday, beautiful girl!" into her ear. Ava felt herself calming and was grateful. She flashed what she knew to be her best smile at Jasmine and replied in a whisper, "Thanks. But you know, to be honest, I'm not at all sure today is our birthday. When I first got here, I think we were having a Tuesday, or something like a Tuesday. And I remember looking forward to my birthday on the coming Friday. But it seems like I've been here for weeks. Can it really be only a few days? Is today even a Friday?"

"Jeepers, Ava, who knows? It's close enough anyway, right? At some point, Louise and Evelyn and you either have turned, or will be turning, twenty-one. Can't we just call it your birthday and get on with the party?"

Ava laughed. "Sure thing, Jas."

Jasmine sashayed through the crowd, vibrant in a metallic silver unitard and hot pink miniskirt spangled with glitter stars. She towed Ava, Harvey, and Lola behind her. The noise of the chatter surrounding them prevented her from talking, so she gestured across the room to where the catering tables had been set up. Ava could see Jack and a beautiful redhead, whom she assumed to be Annie. She and Annie kept missing each other, so Ava was glad to have the chance to meet, but she could tell by Jasmine's expression that Annie had not been the point of her gesture.

"What is it?" Ava asked, leaning down and shouting into Jasmine's left ear.

"See those big boxes hanging behind Jack and Annie, between the Doors?" Jasmine yelled back.

"Yes. What are those things?"

"Listen!" Jasmine waved her arms over her head as though she were directing a pilot toward a runway, and Ava saw Annie wave back. Within seconds, music filled the apartment, and everyone stopped talking to listen. The song was an instrumental jazz piece, played with piano and theremin. It was not a dance tune, but Jasmine bopped along anyway, which excited Lola but worried Harvey, who sometimes got knocked over by Lola's enthusiasm. Ava unhooked Lola's leash so she could run to Jack and Annie.

"It's wonderful, Jas, but how'd you do it?"

"It was Annie. She had the idea of asking the staff at the VC landing tower to help with the party by providing a universal radio and a couple of speakers. Of course, they love Annie and were happy to help. Two of them even came over and set it up for us. They're around here somewhere. I'll have to introduce you. Anyway, they must be pretty satisfied themselves because no one ever thought of using the tower's communications equipment for music."

"But where's the music coming from?"

"This is coming directly to us from Orlon Six. How great is that?"

"Truly great!" Ava agreed as another jazz piece began.

Harvey wandered off to find Evelyn and her date, Beau. Ava had just learned that he and Evelyn were a couple. She waved when she sighted them but stayed close to Jasmine, who was leading her to the food and drinks, the centerpiece of which was a strawberry layer cake as tall as Harvey. Dozens of people whom Ava had never met stopped her to say hello and wish her a happy birthday. By the time Jasmine and Ava reached the catering area, the music had changed to cosmic big band. Ava recognized the style but couldn't place all the instruments. Jack and Annie were dancing while Lola ran circles around them, which got the rest of the party swinging, including the townies who'd never danced in their lives. Ava and Jasmine joined the dancing couple just long enough to say hello and make plans to meet for dinner at Cafe Z the next evening.

The two women selected a plate of curried vegetable pies and two crystal flutes of bubbly, and Jasmine gestured to Ava to follow her again. They ascended the spiral stairs to the balcony, where Ava spotted the three Ms, who were seated at a cafe table eating pies and drinking coffee. For the first time, it occurred to Ava that their surface stillness and silence did not necessarily mean they weren't talking.

Jasmine eschewed the cafe tables and chairs that the VC had lent her for the party and guided Ava to one of the red divans nestled against the wall between two of the Doors.

"From here, we can see everything," Jasmine explained. "I like to watch people, don't you?"

Ava nodded and glanced over at the three Ms again. "I think they do too."

"Sure thing," Jasmine answered. "I would introduce you properly, Ava, but the Ms don't operate like that. They've been with us forever, but we don't really know them. We sometimes speak to them directly, but they never respond vocally. They listen to what we have to say, and then go back to their office and write a response, which they print on their ditto machine. They do share the ditto machine, so if we have something formal to say, we print copies too. That's how Sol and Sid and Evelyn and Angie prepared the Music Request for us after we got fed up with the record players they'd built disappearing.

"Most of us believe the Ms are in deeper and more constant communication with the town than the rest of us are. Sometimes, we wonder if they *are* the town—its human face, if you see what I mean.

"Of course, Evelyn would mock that or any idea that recognizes our shared humanity." Jasmine scowled. "I do know that it's obvious that some of us aren't human and, under most circumstances, I'll happily admit it. But that girl gets under my illustrated skin sometimes."

Ava laughed through a mouthful of pie. "Yes, I know. Like me, she lacks tact and has a tone-deaf sense of humor. Unlike me, Evelyn isn't affected much by what others think of her. I've never had that luxury."

"I'm glad you aren't like her. I like you just as you are."

"Likewise, Boop," Ava replied.

"Though, speaking of liking you just as you are, it seems to me that you aren't just the same as you were. The

Ava who went into the infinity pool is a bit different from the Ava who came out of it, wouldn't you say?"

"You can tell?"

Jasmine nodded while raising her glass of bubbly to Ava. "Here's to the new you. It's an upgrade, I believe." She winked.

Ava stared at her. "What do you mean?"

"You seem more relaxed and confident. I've even heard you make a couple of attempts at jokes."

"*Hmm*," Ava answered, and then stared downward, across the long gallery and toward the front door.

Jasmine didn't pretend she didn't know what or who was still missing from the party.

"How do you feel, Ava, waiting for her?"

Ava sat up straight and locked eyes with Jasmine. "Can you read my mind too? I didn't think you could do that."

"No, of course not. I can't read anybody's mind, not even Julie's." Jasmine glanced down at the dancing crowd, quickly finding her lookalike, who was dressed in a belted, acid-yellow tunic and black leather thigh boots. "Even though we look like twins, we have nothing else in common. Except for pancakes. We both love pancakes."

Watching Julie bouncing around the dance floor, Ava suspected the two women had more in common than pancakes, but she kept this to herself. "Wow, that music is something. What do you call that? Outer space techno-pop?" Ava didn't recognize the songs, but they sounded like house music from the clubs back home. "Are you sure this is coming from Orlon Six and not L.A.?"

"No, I'm not sure. Jack is our DJ, so he's in charge of finding the stations. He said the jazz was Orlon Six, but this could be Galactica Five or, yeah, maybe L.A. That would be a hoot, huh?"

Ava laughed. "Shouldn't we be hearing from their DJs?"

"No, the stations could be fully automated. Or, it's their bedtime, and they left music playing while they're off the air. We're light years away from them, so who knows? Jack wouldn't choose stations with DJs hosting, anyway. Talking would interrupt the party. Plus, it would require a universal translator assembly, which we didn't request from the tower."

Ava nodded, wondering how such a translator would work.

"Now, stop avoiding the subject, Ava. You seem a little bit, I don't know, filled with nervous anticipation maybe?"

Ava sighed and sat back in her chair, draining her glass of bubbly. "No, it's not that . . ." she began.

Annie approached with a chilled bottle of sparkling wine and refilled their glasses. "You two keep this bottle. It's Galactica Five's best. Here, Ava, this is for you." Annie passed Ava a glossy, cream-colored envelope with her name scrawled across the front in black ink. Ava turned it over to see a wax seal embossed with the familiar three-hares-on-a-pie symbol. "One came for Evelyn too. Harvey is bringing it to her."

"Thanks, Annie. Who brought them?" Ava asked.

"One of the staff over at the VC, who couldn't come to the party, sent a messenger over," Annie replied. Seeing Ava's expression, she added, "I hope it's good news, or at least not bad news. I'll leave you two alone." She kissed Ava's head gently and moved on to the three Ms' table to deliver a fresh pot of coffee.

Ava laid the envelope by her side and drank down another half glass of bubbly, while Jasmine watched her.

"Hey, you need to slow down there a little, blondie. You don't usually drink, do you?"

Ava shook her head. "No, I don't. It makes me act weird."

Jasmine didn't laugh. She could see that Ava was trying to hold herself together.

"What are you doing to yourself then? What's wrong? And why aren't you opening that letter?"

"I don't need to open it. I know what it says." Ava finished off her glass and immediately refilled it. "She's not coming."

"Louise? She's not coming to your birthday?" Jasmine reached out and took Ava's nearest hand in her own.

"No, she's not," Ava replied. "But it's okay. I already knew. I knew all along. Well, at least since the pool happened. I could just feel it, and I'm sure Evelyn could too. We wanted to believe Lolo's message that Jack passed on to us, and I'm sure she meant it herself when she announced her intentions to the VC tower, but we both knew we weren't going to see her again. By now, she's back home in California."

Ava looked down onto the main floor, where Evelyn was standing straight and still among the dancers, looking up at her. When Ava met her eyes, Evelyn blew her a kiss, which Ava pretended to catch. She turned her attention back to Jasmine.

"We'll be fine. In a way, it's for the best. Mom was missing us, and Lolo will be there to celebrate our birthday with her. And you're right, Jas, I should open this." She tore open the envelope, and out fluttered two orange paper cranes, which swooped around her head screeching, "Happy Birthday!" and "Welcome home!" for several seconds before bursting into flames. Jasmine and Ava jumped to their feet and began looking around frantically for anything they could use to put out the fire.

"It's okay! Everything's fine up here! No need to worry!" Jasmine yelled. She was splashing bubbly into the air to douse the birds, but the crowd on the main floor hadn't noticed. They were too high on music, dancing, and bubbly to worry about anything.

Ava watched, bemused and saddened to see her delicate birthday gifts from Lolo reduced to bits of ash, which floated down to land at her feet, some of them clinging to her sandals. Jack kept the crowd distracted by pumping up the volume on a song that was impossible to sit through, while Annie and blue-haired Angie began circulating the last of the food and telling everyone they'd be cutting the cake soon.

Broussard had spent most of the evening stalking Jasmine from a discreet distance so that no one would notice him. He disliked crowds, distrusted strangers, and wanted to be near his roommate. His low-profile maneuvers had been going well until the sight of the swooping cranes made him forget himself. He bounded from his hiding place behind a potted lemon tree on the balcony, heading straight for the paper birds. He reached them just in time to receive a dousing of bubbly from Jasmine, who was splattering it everywhere except on her targets.

"Sorry, Broussy, I didn't see you there," Jasmine explained. The cat sauntered over to the divan and leaped onto a cushion, where he proceeded to give himself a thorough cleaning.

"Oh, my stars, it's a cat!" Evelyn shrieked and took off running toward the stairs. Broussard was too distracted by his soggy tail to notice Evelyn's approach. She'd scooped him up into a crushing cuddle before he'd even realized what was happening. "He's perfect, Jasmine! Where'd you get him?"

"I didn't exactly 'get him,' Evelyn. He's a free spirit. But since you asked, he came through that Door right behind you."

"He came through a Door? Are you serious?" Evelyn asked.

"Would I tease you about something like that, Evelyn?"

"I don't know, would you?"

Jasmine hesitated before admitting, "Yes, I probably would, come to think of it. Just to watch the smoke rising out of your ears while you tried to figure out whether I was joking."

"My ears have never once smoked," Evelyn replied huffily, holding Broussard at arm's length as though he were an infant with a soggy diaper. Broussard began to struggle.

Jasmine sighed. "Ava? Would you talk to her?"

"It's true, Evy. That is Broussard's Door right behind you, that blue one. Don't you see the cat flap there at the bottom?"

Evelyn peered down at the Door and, seeing that the flap was just about cat-sized, dropped Broussard to the ground. Broussard scuttled under the divan.

"Hey! Be careful with him!" Jasmine scowled at Evelyn, who bristled.

"If I'd had any idea you were opening Doors and letting things creep in, I never would have picked him up in the first place. My stars! We have no idea where he's been, what kind of diseases he might be carrying, or what he might become when our backs are turned."

"Yeah, okay, I know," Jasmine replied, too tired and tipsy to fight this battle. Besides, Evelyn was not alone in her fear of things coming through Doors. It was shared by the whole town. "But he's a good boy. He's lived with me off and on for a while now, and we're friends. Besides, I think he's had a tough time wherever he came from because, sometimes, we can hear screaming from the other side."

"Are you saying you've adopted the cat of a psycho from another world? Jasmine, I'm not sure you've thought this through logically."

"Maybe not, but Broussard is my buddy, and I'm not sending him home. He is welcome to stay here, for however long he wants." Jasmine walked over to Ava, who was crouched near the railing of the balcony, staring at the pieces of her dead cranes. "And that goes for you, too, tall blonde chick." Jasmine brushed her fingers lightly through Ava's hair.

Ava glanced up, "Sorry, what? I was just . . . Never mind. What goes for me too?"

"You are welcome here at my place anytime, and for however long you want to stay," Jasmine repeated.

Ava smiled. "That's the sweetest invitation I've ever had, Jas."

Evelyn clapped her hands together and spun on her toes, making the skirt of her citrus orange dress twirl like a flower carried on the wind. "Now that is a nice birthday present, you two. It's wonderful to see you together."

She moved toward her friends to embrace them but was stopped short by Ava jumping to her feet and exclaiming, "Look, they're moving! I thought it was the wine affecting me, but it's actually happening, isn't it?"

Evelyn and Jasmine looked down at the ashes which were spinning themselves into a dust devil. As the three of them watched, the mini whirlwind traveled across the floor, collecting every speck of debris that had made up the birds.

Broussard crept out from under the divan and, after checking that Evelyn was not within grabbing distance, sidled up to Jasmine. The women were too entranced by the ash spectacle to notice the cat, who was likewise entranced. Broussard aimed his pounce carefully, so he would not miss his moving target. His magnificent jump landed him squarely on top of the spinning ashes. For a suspended moment or two, there was utter silence from the little group on the balcony, as they bore witness to this second death of the cranes.

"No, no, no!" Ava clasped her hands to her chest and dropped to her knees. "Broussy, what have you done?"

"I'm sorry, Ava," Jasmine said quietly, placing one hand on Ava's shoulder and squeezing it. "I should have known he would do that. I'm still getting used to cats."

"He does seem very pouncy," Evelyn added. "Are they all like that, do you think?"

Broussard began to hiss and growl, eventually leaping from his captured prey to crouch behind Jasmine, where he continued to hiss. Jasmine and Evelyn were bickering about cats, with their backs turned to the ash pile, so Ava was the only one of the three who observed the pile growing upward and outward until it was five feet high and resembled a miniature volcano. There was a moment of perfect stillness while she waited, breathless with anticipation.

Jasmine and Evelyn stopped arguing and turned around at the very moment two dusky orange cranes erupted from the volcano's cone, sending ashes flying everywhere. The cranes' trumpeting calls thrilled Ava to her bones. She laughed and applauded as the birds steadied themselves on their feet and readied their wings for flight. The cranes took to the air with grace, their dark legs trailing behind, circling once, twice, then a third time around their mistress, before taking off to explore the cavernous apartment.

"Jeepers, Ava, I feel outdone," Jasmine said. "I made you a dress. Paper cranes that turn into real ones are way cooler."

The women watched as the elegant cranes flew among the guests, exciting an already lively gathering. Ava kept her eyes on the birds and said, "Those are sandhill cranes, a breeding pair from the look of their plumage. We might end up with a family." She turned to Jasmine. "They are a fantastic gift, but I love my dress, too, Jas. Nobody's ever made me a dress before."

"It is a gorgeous dress, Jasmine," Evelyn conceded," and it would look great on either of us."

Jasmine laughed, her annoyance with Evelyn forgotten. "I'm glad you think so because I made you one, too, only it's sea green. It's wrapped and waiting beneath the cake table."

Evelyn beamed and threw her arms around Jasmine. "Thank you, sweet Jasmine! I thought I was going to have to steal Ava's."

"I suspected that which is why you have your own. Hey, what did Lolo send you, by the way?"

Ava turned her attention to Evelyn. "Yes, I was wondering that too. Have you opened it?"

"No, I wanted to do it with you. Is now a good time?"

The three women settled on the divan, with Jasmine in the middle and Broussard on her lap. Evelyn used a sharp orange fingernail to break open the wax seal on the envelope.

"It's a poem," she said, pulling out a single sheet of lilac paper and unfolding it. "Should I read it aloud?"

"Please," Ava answered. "Otherwise, Jasmine won't be able to follow."

"Right. It's going to be familiar anyway. Or, maybe it won't. I mean, it would be if you were ever a child—"

"Oh, my stars! Evelyn Louise, just read the poem," Ava snapped.

"All right, don't get your petticoat in a twist, Ava darlin'. It's a nursery rhyme called the *Three Little Kittens*, by Mother Goose, who may have been a mother, but I'm pretty sure she was never a goose. Here we go." Evelyn cleared her throat and began reading.

The three little kittens, they lost their mittens,
And they began to cry,
'Oh, mother dear, we sadly fear,
That we have lost our mittens.'
'What! Lost your mittens, you naughty kittens!
Then you shall have no pie.'
'Meow, meow, meow.'
'Then you shall have no pie.'
The three little kittens, they found their mittens,
And they began to cry,
'Oh, mother dear, see here, see here,
For we have found our mittens.'
'Put on your mittens, you silly kittens,
And you shall have some pie.'
'Purr, purr, purr,
Oh, let us have some pie.'

She stopped reading and turned over the paper. "That's it. That's all she wrote."

"That's *it*?" Jasmine asked, reaching for the paper, which Evelyn handed to her. "What kind of stupid present is that?" Jasmine looked ready to be offended on Evelyn's behalf, but she noticed that Ava and Evelyn were looking at each other and smiling as if they shared a secret. "Okay, what am I missing, you two?"

"*Shh*," Ava whispered, "listen."

"What? I don't hear anything but party music."

Broussard, though, did hear. He leaped from Jasmine's lap and disappeared under the divan, returning moments later with a mewling ball of fur in his teeth. He made the trip two more times until Evelyn's lap held a trio of chocolate and beige kittens with mismatched eyes, seal-point markings, and cream mittens for paws.

"I have to credit Lolo for knowing how to choose perfect gifts," Jasmine said. "I'll find you a basket for the kitties. For the time being, use this." She pulled a cover off one of the divan pillows and passed it to Evelyn, who bundled up her triplets with an extreme gentleness that Ava had never seen in her. "I've been ordering cat supplies from my vendor, so I can give you everything you need."

Evelyn leaned her left ear toward the kittens before glancing up at Ava and Jasmine. "Do you hear what they're saying?"

"What?" Ava took this question seriously, believing herself increasingly proficient in cat language.

"It sounds like '*Purr, purr, purr*—Oh, let us have some pie.'"

Twenty-One

Ava had begged Jasmine to forgo speeches and birthday songs, so the cake was cut and passed around with a minimum of fanfare. Jack adjusted the radio to a mild ambient station, and everyone gathered into groups to visit for a while before heading home. He and Annie joined their friends on the balcony.

The group had pulled some tables together and were enjoying the last of the cake and wine when a soft banging began on one of the Doors. The banging increased rapidly in volume and intensity until every partygoer had turned to stare at it. Someone turned off the music, and the entire gallery fell silent. The three Ms made their way over to where the group made up of Jack, Annie, Beau, Evelyn, Jasmine, and Harvey sat.

"Jack?" Annie said, looking over at her husband, who was rising to his feet.

"Oh, my stars," Evelyn whispered. "Look." The rest of their group rose abruptly and began moving toward the blue Door, where the sound was coming from, but they were farther away than the heedless girl aiming straight for it. Ava had wandered off to the bathroom a while ago, after finishing off the bottle of Galactica Five bubbly. Now, oblivious to the hushed crowd and the alarm on her friends' faces, she was trotting up the balcony stairs with the intention of greeting the newcomer. Whatever was on the other side continued to alternate between furious banging and hurling its weight against the wood, but the Door held.

"Who is it?" Ava yelled, reaching for the silver knob without waiting for a response. "Well, whoever you are, welcome to our party!"

She managed to swing the Door open wide, just before passing out cold.

* * *

Two days later, just before sunrise, Ava and Jasmine were lying in Jasmine's loft while she recapped the party's climax for Ava, whose last memory of the night was watching Evelyn swaddle her kittens tenderly in soft fabric.

"Yeah, so then you yelled, 'Who is it?' Like some monster was going to announce its name and that he'd come to eat us, right? Then, before any of us could stop you, you screamed, 'Welcome to our party!' and threw open the Door."

"I did that?" Ava was incredulous.

"Sure thing, blondie. You acted like you were greeting your best friend, only we had no idea what was trying to get in. Then you fainted. Very gracefully, for what it's worth. You just kind of dropped to the ground in a heap. The intruder blundered in and fell right on top of you."

"Oh, no."

"Yep. By that point, Beau, who as you know is the size of a refrigerator, had reached the Door, and Jack was right behind him. They tackled this poor guy while Evelyn and I pulled you out of the way. This fellow, who's no taller than me and way skinnier, was so terrified I thought he was going to pass out too. And by the way, I totally believe you now about being even weirder than usual when you drink alcohol. It's all fruit juice from here on out, right?"

"But who was he, Jas?" Ava sat up and leaned against the wall, glancing down at the pink Zoom-the-Moon Grocers t-shirt she was wearing. It had the shop's name and the cute spaceship logo printed on it, both in lime green. "Hey, nice shirt! Can I keep it?"

"Sure thing. I'd be offended if you didn't. By the way, Harvey is looking after the cranes while you recover. He has them with him at the motel, and they love the infinity pool."

Broussard, who'd been sleeping at the foot of the bed, moved closer to Ava and rubbed his face against her hands. Ava scratched his chin.

"Broussy has been worried about you too. He's probably never seen anyone sleep so long. I don't think I have either."

"How long have I been asleep?"

"Two nights and a full day. You conked out the night of the party and slept all day yesterday, and now it's morning again, just. The sun's about to rise. I had to cancel our dinner with Jack and Annie. I told them we'd reschedule when you were conscious. I wasn't too worried though since you did warn us that you tended to take longer than normal to sleep off a hangover." She poured Ava another glass of water from the pitcher she'd brought up to the loft, and Ava gulped it down.

"Thanks. I'm sorry about scaring everybody. But the guy turned out to be okay, from the sound of it?"

"Yes, he's good. He's staying with Jack and Annie until he gets oriented."

"You mean he's staying here permanently?"

"Looks like it. His name is Garland and, as it turns out, his apartment is—or was—connected to mine through a super-long corridor that reached from his hall closet to the blue Door. I think the corridor must be conceptual rather than actual, though, because Broussard entered from the void, as I mentioned when you first met him."

"It was Broussard's Door?"

"Exactly. Garland and his ex-girlfriend were Broussard's family: the girlfriend being the screamer we've been hearing off and on. They broke up recently, and she kept the apartment and Broussy. She just wanted to be malicious, Garland said, because she doesn't even like cats. He'd come back to reclaim Broussard when he learned that she'd tossed him into a hall closet and locked the door. Garland was incensed at that point but more worried about the cat than battling it out with a lunatic who abuses animals. He opened their hall door, and guess what?"

"What?"

"It was a solid wall."

"What?"

"The cupboard was bare," Jasmine explained. "Not really, but I've always wanted to say that. The interior of the closet just wasn't there anymore. It was a blank wall made of the same plasterboard as the rest of their hallway. The door opened to nothing and nowhere."

"How peculiar."

"Yeah, and his ex, Lydia, started screaming about her winter coats and shoes, which she kept in that closet. Garland ran outside and rifled through the trunk of his car until he found his hatchet."

"A hatchet?" Ava asked. "What kind of person keeps a hatchet in his trunk?"

"Annie asked the same question, but Garland explained that he hadn't unpacked everything after moving because his new studio is small. He's from a place called Minnesota. Have you ever heard of it?"

"Yes. It gets bitterly cold there and snows a lot. And they have moose."

"That's what he said, too, except for the part about the moose. What's a moose?"

"I'll tell you later."

"Okay. Anyway, he said that Lydia looked terrified when he came running back into the apartment with the hatchet—like she thought he was going all Jack Nicholson on her . . . Who's Jack Nicholson?"

"Later. Finish the story!"

"Okay. All Garland wanted to do was find his cat. He started hacking away at the wall while Lydia, who'd figured out by then that he wasn't planning to chop her to bits, berated him the entire time about losing the deposit on the apartment. Once the opening was big enough, Garland crawled through into the corridor and kept right on walking. That's how he ended up here."

"Wow."

"I know, crazy story, right? What's even crazier though is that I think Broussard and Garland's Door is gone. I woke up yesterday and wandered over to check on things. When I reached down to latch the cat flap, my fingers hit a solid wall. There's no corridor, no void, and no sound coming through." Jasmine shifted to the edge of the bed and stepped onto the ladder of the loft. "Come on down, and I'll make us some breakfast. I want to show you something special."

"Good, I'm starving." Ava watched as Broussard leaped to the ground, bypassing the ladder entirely. "I wish I could do that, Broussy, but I might break something," she said and followed Jasmine down to the open lounge of the apartment. "Is Garland happy about staying here? It doesn't sound like he has a choice."

"He's thrilled. He's a small-town kind of guy, and his only real loves are books and cats. He's a librarian, and we happen to need of one of those."

"That's perfect. I'd forgotten about the library. I haven't been there yet."

"There isn't much to see. The rooms are nice-looking and fully equipped but lacking one crucial thing."

"Let me guess. Books were left out of the original design?" Ava laughed, following Jasmine into the kitchen.

"That would be the problem, yes. The only ones we have are some cheap paperbacks that tourists from off-world left behind." Jasmine pretended to be counting books on her fingers as she named the titles. "I've read *The Lost Horizon of Oolong-Ree*, *Peyton Place Pandemonium*, *Valley of the Screaming Headless Dolls*, and *Last Exit to Orlon Six* at least a dozen times each. Reading only four books over a lifetime that moves as slow as mine has left a big gap in my learning. We could do with some fresh material, is my point. Now that we have a bona fide librarian in town, he can stock it for us. Maybe you can help too? You like books, right?"

"Yes, but I read books on ecology and birds, mostly. I can help stock the science shelves, though."

"I can set up the off-world vendors for him through the broker who organizes my grocery suppliers for me." Jasmine started the coffee brewing and popped bread into the toaster, then turned to Ava. "Now, do you notice anything different?"

Ava was slipping on a pair of jeans from an overnight bag that Evelyn had dropped off for her, and had hardly bothered to take in her setting.

"Oh, my stars!" Jasmine's apartment had converted itself back into the high-ceilinged, single-story dwelling over the shop that it appeared to be from the outside. The enormous room with its spiral staircases, overhanging balcony, and glass roof was gone. The Doors, too, were gone, along with the blue silk curtains, and presumably the cosmos-viewing deck. All that remained were the cozy domestic rooms and furnishings that had been tucked into the corner of the vast gallery. "This is nice, Jas. Very homey."

"Thanks. I hoped you'd like it. This is how I like to live most of the time, but I do have to keep an eye on the Doors. Whenever I want to convert the place, I push the *PITS* button over the sink, and off we go.

"Pits?"

"It's all capitals: *P-I-T-S* is an acronym for *Pie in the Sky*," Jasmine explained.

Ava remembered her blackbird friend and ran over to the front door, which was the same glossy red as usual. When she opened it, the stenciled bird perched on the painted twig beneath the brass knocker fluttered its wings and twittered.

"He's still there," Jasmine said. "But come look at this." She was standing in front of three tall, narrow windows that looked out over the street.

Ava joined her, assuming she wanted to share the experience of a particularly gorgeous desert sunrise since the apartment faced east. Instead, Jasmine stepped behind Ava, took hold of her shoulders, and turned her toward the south end of town, where the motel was.

"Can you see it? I thought it might be the right time by now," Jasmine said.

Ava gasped and clapped her hands. "Yes, I can see it. I can see all of it, and it's fantastic!"

The main building of the visitor center lit up the block behind Cafe Z, Rocket Records, and Cinema Retrograde like a 1950s-space-age fantasy, while its smaller counterparts shone like neon beacons against the desert sand. Ava could see air traffic buzzing around the area and hear voices coming from loudspeakers. Jasmine pointed out the landing pads for cargo and tourist ships, which required special assistance and guided descents from the control tower. Small personal vehicles, she explained, could land almost anywhere, without any help.

"The main building—that big one that's been modeled on the old-style spaceships—is the welcome center, and that tall spire shooting up behind it is the communications tower. The other places dotted around out there include one luxury-style hotel catering to couples, an economy hotel, a restaurant that most of us locals avoid, a garage that handles repairs, and a family fun center that has pizza, miniature golf, and roller skating. I'll take you there sometime."

"Is that the Infinite Loop?" Ava asked, pointing to the biggest roller coaster she'd ever seen, which rested alone out in the desert like an old dinosaur. It was farther to the southeast than the VC or the motel and at least two miles from town, by Ava's estimate. The sun was still waking up, so the lights surrounding the coaster hadn't switched off yet. Ava could see the bright white wood and the fire-engine-red tracks clearly. It looked just like the kind of coaster that Jeannie searched for whenever they visited an amusement park, only way bigger.

"That's the Infinite Loop, dear girl, and as you can see, the track ends in the sky."

"Oh. I thought maybe it reversed backward at that point."

"Nope. You just keep going. The Loop is a launching pad that can send you off to anywhere in the universe you'd care to go. If you want a holiday that promises you the 'time of your life,' the Loop is where you board your touring ship. They seat up to four people. Ever since Rachel and Lenie discovered the Loop, we rarely see them here at home. They no sooner return than they are off again. Still, that's understandable, given that the hope of forever holidays is where the whole Pie Town dream began for them." Jasmine took Ava's left hand in her right and squeezed it gently. "What about you? You want to shoot off in an apple-green spaceship for the time of your life?"

Ava smiled and kissed her. "I think I'll keep my ship right here with you, Jas. I'm already having the time of my life. I can't imagine it gets better than this."

Epilogue

Ava and Harvey reclined side-by-side near the infinity pool, watching the cranes eat from the bowl of grains and berries Ava had set out for them. She was working on a design for a patch of wetlands in Skylights Park, which the three Ms had agreed to implement. In the meantime, Felix and Felicity seemed happy relaxing with Harvey at the motel. The pool had helpfully transformed itself into fresh water and installed an assortment of grasses, reeds, and lily pads for the birds to enjoy.

Ava was still trying to get used to Harvey's burgeoning friendship with the cat vines, his favorite of which had draped itself around his neck and kept knocking his reading glasses askew. Harvey insisted the cat vines' aggression was just their way of playing, but neither Ava nor Evelyn trusted them. Evelyn had completely lost interest in them since getting real kittens and was careful to keep her triplets out of the courtyard where the vines grew. Most especially, the women did not trust this one, Vera, as Harvey called her. How he knew Vera was female was a mystery. Ava kept stealing glances at the six furry tendrils coiled beneath Harvey's lounger, just to make sure they stayed there; but the two tendrils sharpening their claws on the bark of the tree directly behind her head were even more unnerving. Then again, if she couldn't trust Harvey's judgment, whose could she trust? Ava tried to relax and refocus her attention on the sky, which was endlessly captivating.

The superhighway was busy tonight. Little ships, sparkling like gems, darted here and there. Some continued on their way to New Mexico or California or Alpha Centauri.

Others landed in the parking lot behind the diner, where they transformed instantly into rusty old cars, trucks, and campers. The occupants, looking like music festival groupies, wandered inside for a slice of the best pie in the universe and bottomless cups of fresh coffee.

Simultaneously, Ava and Harvey reached out for one another, and she took his paw in her hand, ignoring the hiss from Vera, who tended to be possessive. Life was good, she thought, but it would be even better if they had some pie about now. Harvey nodded, and they both got to their feet for a stroll to the diner.

Ava had become accustomed to running most of her random theories and ideas past her friend whenever they were together, so she didn't hesitate to consult him when an essential piece of the cosmic puzzle revealed itself to her over a slice of coconut meringue. "Harvey, do you suppose that the real secret of the universe is that it runs entirely on pie?"

About the Authors

Sandra Peterson Ramirez and td Whittle have been friends for most of their lives, although they live in separate hemispheres these days. Between them, they have had dozens of small jobs and two lengthy professional careers, including restaurants, retail, bookselling, publishing, tech support, computer programming, electronics assembly, and family therapy. Both have been avid readers and book collectors since childhood. More of their writing and photography can be found on their website, *Like Telling the Truth* http://www.liketellingthetruth.com